BEST
GAY EROTICA
OF THE YEAR

VOLUME TWO

BEST
GAY EROTICA
OF THE YEAR

VOLUME TWO

WARLORDS & WARRIORS

Edited by

ROB ROSEN

CLEiS
PRESS

Published in the United States by Cleis Press, an imprint of Start Midnight, LLC, 101 Hudson Street, 37th Floor, Suite 3705, Jersey City, NJ 07302

Printed in the United States.
Cover design: Scott Idleman/Blink
Cover photograph: Dreamstime
Text design: Frank Wiedemann
First Edition.
10 9 8 7 6 5 4 3 2 1

Trade paper ISBN: 978-1-62778-190-9
E-book ISBN: 978-1-62778-191-6

For Kenny,
my blue-eyed conquering hero

CONTENTS

INTRODUCTION

Roman legionaries, Britannic thieves, Egyptian royal guards, Vikings and barbarians and every sort of dashing warrior in between spill from the following adventure-teeming pages with tales of battles both past and future. Revel in the heart-pounding victories, sob at the wretched defeats, but, more importantly, immerse yourself in the steaming erotic encounters between enemies and allies alike, of men conquering men both on the field and in their beds.

Rhidian Brenig Jones temptingly starts us off with "Athene Noctua," where our Roman hero finds himself held captive by the Silures, until captivity becomes a willing threesome you won't soon forget. Mortal enemies turned lovers grace the pages of Salome Wilde's "To the Victor," while Evey Brett offers us the impossibly beautiful and harrowing tale of feudal Japanese warriors in "Dragon's Son." Brent Archer tells of a Viking battle with barbarian Picts in "The Orkney Landing," and of two lovers adding a third to their lives, while Eric Del Carlo thrills us with "A Time for Thieves," the guard in the story, of all things, a sexy albino. In between, read of a Greek and a Thracian prince, Revolutionary War Tories and Patriots, a Moldavian king, Gothic barbarians, Warsaw Ghetto resistance fighters, and, to finish it all off, the hauntingly original and futuristic "Mojave," by famed erotica writer Dale Chase.

With a backdrop of sweeping vistas and fields bloody with battle, of remote deserts and landscapes long forgotten, the stories that follow are intricately woven, beautifully rendered and always of the highest literary caliber. In short, this collection is sure to have something for everyone!

Enjoy and happy reading,

Rob Rosen
San Francisco

ATHENE NOCTUA

Rhidian Brenig Jones

Dark. The smell of smoke. The light of a lamp falling on his face, hurting his eyes. A flinch, and the pain biting like an axe buried, rocking into bone. A wail breaking from his chest.

An arm supporting his shoulders. "Drink, Roman." The clink of a cup against his teeth and a bitter mouthful, spraying as he coughed.

"Do you need to make water?" Something cold pushing between his thighs and the helpless gush of voiding.

The glimmer of a hearth, and the redder agony in his head receding as the kindly dark reclaimed him.

"Ah, you return to us."

Lucius came to his senses in a round room, its curving walls whitewashed and painted with flowing patterns, spirals and coils in blue and green. A table. Stools. A column of smoke wafted into a thatched ceiling, bending now and again in a draft from the door.

A stout man, blunt-featured, his sparse white hair braided,

unfolded his hands from a comfortable belly. "How does your head feel—ah, quiet now, quiet now! Pointless to pull against the ropes." The world spun and Lucius sank back, a spurt of vomit sour in his throat. Under a brightly colored blanket he was naked and spread-eagled, tied by his wrists and ankles to the cot. Knowing fingers searched and probed the cropped curls at the back of his head. "Legionaries are renowned as doughty fighters, but, by the gods, they're hardheaded, too. You have a lump like a duck's egg, but no break, I think. My name is Aneirin. What's yours?"

Lucius stared rigidly, his teeth clenched against the sickness that threatened to unman him.

"Yes, well...come, a sip of this will settle a queasy stomach." The cot creaked, sagging dangerously under the old man's bulk. He swirled the liquid in the cup. "Poison is not our way, *decanus*. This is only willow bark and ginger, with a drop of honey, no poppy this time. No? You're sure? As you wish. It'll keep for my poor knees. Ah, Nesta, there you are."

A woman with a face like a frog hobbled toward them, a small pot in her hand. She muttered something in their hateful language and elbowed Aneirin out of her way.

"Nesta brings the pot for you to make water again." Seeing Lucius's expression, Aneirin said blandly, "She has swaddled five sons and their sons, too. I doubt a Roman cock will hold much terror for her. Or you can piss yourself and lie in it. It makes no odds."

The woman lifted away the cloth from Lucius's hips. She took his cock between finger and gnarled thumb and hung it over the rim of the pot. Once she was satisfied with its placing, she stared into the fire until Lucius had finished. She shook him perfunctorily, then peered into the pot and held it out for Aneirin's inspection. He nodded, dismissing her.

"There is no blood in your water," he remarked.

Lucius's face burned. He was beyond humiliation.

2

Aneirin drew up a stool. "I learned your language in Rome, as a young man. Your countrymen are not renowned for their manners, but I found her citizens courteous enough. That's the privilege of the conqueror, of course. Nonetheless, I've given you my name; won't you give me yours?" He paused, but Lucius lay as dumb as a stone. Perhaps his stubborn silence stung Aneirin, because he declared flatly, "Your comrades, the seven, are dead."

The accursed rain had finally stopped and the scouting party, tired after a grueling day in the hills, lay wrapped in sodden cloaks. Scudding clouds revealed the moon, its light silvering Dulius's spear point as he kept the watch. The silence was only broken by drips from the trees and the eerie shrieks of a distant vixen. Lucius tucked his chin into his chest and wished that he had the discipline of his tent mates, who had instantly fallen asleep. Thoughts of home drifted through his mind. Thoughts of the sun, diamond bright on blue seas. Of Marcellus. Marcellus...his iron-gray hair and iron-hard prick. He sighed and pushed away from the rock. If sleep wouldn't come, he might as well share the watch. He reached for his sword. In that instant, a figure rose smoothly behind Dulius. Gorgon headed and terrible, it opened the man's throat with one slash of a blade.

Lucius surged to his feet, roaring the battle cry, but it was lost in the screams of the demons who erupted from the trees, spears jabbing, murderous knives plunging. Without armor, with no shield and his head bare, he whirled into the melee, but before he could strike, a stunning blow to the back of his skull dropped him to his knees. He swayed, his sword falling from his fist as he pitched forward into the mud.

"Did you think you could pass through our lands without us knowing? That we were blind to the rats in the grain pits? We'd been watching you for days." He patted Lucius's thigh, making him jerk against his bindings. "You showed courage. No shame to you that we fought better."

But shame crushed him. The heads of his comrades would now be rotting under the leaden skies of Cambria, nailed to trees or jouncing from triumphant saddles. Gap-toothed Marcus. Handsome, cool-eyed Antoninus. Lucullus, grabbing his balls and boasting that he'd leave the most leathery old whore in Isca bowlegged and whimpering after one night on his cock. No brothels for Lucullus now, none of the delights of Corinium. No whores, pox ridden or otherwise. And none for him, either. The men from the southlands of Germania were expensive, but he believed the talk he'd heard, that they were worth every last piece of silver they charged. They understood the hunger that gnawed and they fed it—ah, with their thick, oiled cocks they fed it, even if the appetite grew with the feeding.

"Aren't you wondering why you're still alive and the others dead, *decanus*? Your lumpy head is still on your shoulders, slingshot or no." Aneirin reached out and touched the amulet that lay on Lucius's breast, the baby charm that he still liked to wear, despite his comrades' jeers. Marcellus had sucked the little golden owl that night in Tibur.

He had wondered, and wondered with dread. The taverns of Isca had been rife with tales of the inventiveness of the Silures in designing death for soldiers unlucky enough to survive the field of battle. Flaying. White-hot rods thrust into the openings of the body. Boiling in cauldrons. Sweat blistered his hairline and his mouth dried. But he met the old man's eyes steadily enough.

"There in the valley, when you lay senseless and the warriors were about to slit your throat, they saw this." Aneirin touched the charm again, with reverence. "Arianrhod's owl. You know her as Minerva, of course, but the goddess has many names. It's a sign that you're under her protection—for now. But her silver wheel is turning. Pray that when it stops you're not broken beneath it." He sighed. "Are you hungry? I have some good bread and new cheese—" He cocked an ear. The clopping of hooves cantering to a halt outside the house brought him to his feet. "A moment."

With every ounce of strength in his back, Lucius strained against the ropes. Veins stood out on his temples and red spots danced before his eyes, but the bindings only tightened and cut into his skin. His head spinning, almost howling with frustrated fury, he fell back and listened to the excited hubbub outside. *Arianrhod? Some ugly bitch goddess of these savages.*

"You still wear a bulla." Amused, Marcellus drew the chain from Lucius's tunic and let the warmed charm dangle.

"Laugh if you like, everyone does, but I like it."

Marcellus touched a knuckle to Lucius's jaw, where the down of a boy was coarsening into the beard of a man. "Ah, little owl, you're fledging." Gray eyes gazed into marigold, into the bright eyes that had given Lucius his nickname, but the older man dropped his hand and turned abruptly away. This high in the hills, the late evening air was cool, freshened by the cascades of sweet water that made the summer villas of Tibur so popular, far as they were from the festering stinks of Rome. He looked up at the stars. "The gods order men's lives with great cruelty."

"What do you mean?"

"If they'd truly favored us, we'd have been born Greek."

"Why would you want us to be born Greek?"

"You know very well why. Don't tease, Lucius, I'm not in the mood for it."

Lucius got up from the couch and joined Marcellus at the window. They had had this conversation many times, and always to no avail—his luck to be in love with a principled man! He touched the broad shoulder, the tough curve of muscle of a seasoned tribune, and heat leaped through the linen. "Marcellus, nobody need know."

"I would know and so would you. We'd know that we'd dishonored each other."

"Dishonored each other? By loving? How can you say that?" He took Marcellus's hand and pulled him around to face him. "Kiss me, then. Only a kiss, if it's all you can give."

"Kiss you?" Marcellus swallowed hard. "I want to do more than kiss you. All shame to me."

"No shame. You're a good man, an honorable man, and I love you for it."

He smiled tightly. "I don't feel very good and honorable at the moment."

Lucius pressed his hand to the center of Marcellus's chest and felt the thumping beat of that great heart. "Tell Felix and the other slaves to leave us alone. Please?"

With a troubled look, Marcellus walked to the door and opened it, calling out as he did so and pulling it shut behind him. Lucius could just make out Felix's anxious squeak and his master's gruff response. No doubt the fussy soul would be wanting to clear away the remains of the supper and bring oil for the lamps. Night was falling fast. It had been a fine supper—pork cheeks and fat dormice, mullet, pears and honey cakes—although Marcellus had eaten sparingly, as he always did. The door opened and he came back into the room. Lucius kicked away the soft woolen folds that had pooled at his feet and stood naked, his strong young cock rearing erect from a cloud of black hair. Carefully, Marcellus closed the door and leaned against it, his head bowed and his hands behind his back. He looked up and, for an instant, Lucius saw the face that his battle captains saw when they waited, steady in serried ranks, for his command. He walked to Lucius and gently, so gently, kissed his brow.

"So be it, then, little owl. So be it."

Lucius smiled and spread his thighs and opened his mouth for the kiss.

* * *

Two men swept in, Aneirin behind them.

"So this is our guest."

The same abysmal dress as Aneirin—breeches colored with faint stripes, tunics gathered at the waist with broad belts—but the nearer wore a heavy torc of twisted gold strands and a fine gold circlet on his dark hair. Multiple braids pulled back from his lean, sculpted face and hung down past his shoulders. The other was fairer and more heavily built, and he studied Lucius with expressionless blue eyes.

The dark-haired man picked a hazelnut out of a bowl and threw it into his mouth. He cracked it with back teeth and spat the shell onto the floor. "What's your name, Roman?" His accent was more pronounced than Aneirin's, but the question was clear enough.

Stonily, Lucius held his gaze.

"Doesn't he speak? Perhaps he's deaf. *What's your name, Roman?*" His lip curled. "Perhaps he's sulking, like a woman all peevish in her moon blood. Are you a woman, Julia Drusilla?"

Lucius paled. Through gritted teeth, he said, "Untie me, barbarian, and I'll give you my name. I'll carve it in your guts."

"Oh ho, a barbarian he calls me! If he really is a *he*. They're tricky these Romans, not to be trusted." He took a step and yanked the blanket from Lucius's hips. Two pairs of eyes lingered on his body, then flicked to his face. The fair man muttered something and they both laughed, but it seemed to Lucius, as he lay, bound in helpless fury, that their laughter was forced and rang with a false note.

"Llyr," Aneirin said, quietly reproachful.

"Aneirin." But he dropped the blanket and spun around and feigned a punch at the fair man. Barking with laughter, they wrestled, each trying to hook the other's feet from under him, but neither managing to do it. Grasping each other's shoulders, they struggled and heaved, staggering around the fire until they knocked into a table and sent a dish crashing to the floor.

"*Llyr!*"

They broke apart and grinned at each other, naughty boys chastised. But their grins faded suddenly, like lights blown out, and, to Lucius's astonishment, they kissed, mouths wide and hungrily seeking. Llyr, for it appeared that this was the barbarian's name, draped his arm around his friend's shoulders. "I'll have it, Roman. Your name or your head. In one hour." They sauntered out, still jostling, still shoving, still kissing.

Aneirin lowered himself painfully to gather up the shards of pottery. "I'd treat Llyr with respect if I were you. He's the king's son and he's proud. Also, he means what he says." He hauled himself to his feet with a groan. "I liked that dish," he said ruefully. "Ah, well. Now then, you must be hungry, but how do you intend to eat your food? Shall I feed it to you? Wouldn't you rather have your hands free? Think you'll need to shit before nightfall? Do you really want Nesta visiting with her pot? Come, tell me your name and I'll release you." He raised a whiskery white eyebrow. "I'll heat water so you can wash..."

Lucius told himself that Llyr's threats would never have broken him, but the offer of a wash, to be clean again...his skin was marbled with mud and dried blood, and although the old woman had been careful, drips of piss had wet his balls. He probably stank. "Lucius Matius Dexion," he said.

Aneirin took a knife from the table and began to saw at the cords. "Listen to me, Lucius Matius. Are you listening? You're free under my parole to walk in the hillfort. If you try to escape, you'll be killed, owl or no owl, and your death will be hard."

"What's going to happen to me?"

The last strands of rope separated and Lucius bit back a groan as he sat up, stiff muscles complaining.

"Hywel the king has a shaking palsy that I can't cure. His son decides such things now. Look, let me rub your joints with some salve. My rosemary salve, this, very good for easing and loosening."

"Who are you? What are you?"

"I? An old man with some small skill as a healer. I listen for Arianrhod's voice and sometimes she is gracious enough to speak to me."

"Llyr and the other one?"

"*Llyr*," Aneirin said, correcting his pronunciation.

"Llyr." The acrid smell of the herb filled his nostrils as Aneirin rubbed a palmful of the ointment into the tendons behind his knees, digging in, then stroking the long thighs. He paused and threw Lucius a glance. "You liked what you saw, didn't you? The two of them?"

Lucius managed a scornful grunt. "The *pathicus* and his concubine? They disgusted me."

"Oh, come now—you couldn't take your eyes off them! I know a man who desires men when I see one." More gently, he said, "Our ways are different from the ways of Rome. We take joy in men loving, free men, equal in age, equal in strength. Llyr and Hafod are loving companions of the heart." He slapped a firm calf muscle and gave Lucius a knowing wink. "And loving companions of the bed, eh?"

Lucius returned a wan smile and gave some thought to this.

It had been four days but the clothes still felt wrong on his skin. His own had been quickly claimed by the women, the good linens and wools cut up to make clothes for children. About his weapons Lucius knew nothing, and he mourned the loss of his grandfather's sword. He walked between the roundhouses, their swooping thatched roofs like upturned baskets, no doubt made to keep out the rain of this northern hellhole. Frowning faces stared down at him from a watchtower. A small girl goggled and ducked behind her mother's skirts, but a knot of boys puffed out their skinny chests and glared in manly challenge. Beyond the palings of the outer ramparts lay cultivated fields and gardens, and farther still, pastureland dotted with small black cattle. He wrapped his hands around the splintery points of the fence and wondered about his fate. There was no one in the place who could speak his language, other than Aneirin and Llyr, and he had no wish to bandy words with *him*. He was fearful, and although he was reluctant to admit it even to himself, he was lonely. He rested his chin on the back of his hands and gazed out at the hills.

"Lucius!"

He turned to see Aneirin plodding toward him, a swarm of children tugging at his sleeves.

"Off you go, now, off you go! *Eirlys*!"

A woman rose from her quern-stone and swatted them away from the old man, delivering a smart clout to one boy's head when he aimed a resentful kick at her legs. She held long hair away from her face and looked at Lucius with dark almond eyes before she turned and herded the whining children away.

Aneirin said. "Pretty girl, don't you think?"

Indeed she was, full breasted and plump assed, with a pleasing sway to her walk.

"Pretty enough."

"Oh yes, many a cock raises its head when Eirlys walks by. But..." Aneirin studied the clean lines of the young Roman's profile, the clear amber eyes, the curve of full lips and the stubborn chin.

"What?"

"But it would take a good, hard body and a handsome face to stiffen yours, wouldn't it?"

Lucius's knuckles whitened on the palings.

"Ah, well, that's as may be. I've come to tell you something." He raised an arm and pointed. "Do you see there, at the bottom of the hill? The pastureland?"

"Yes."

"Valuable land that, but as you see, no herds grazing. That's because our neighbors to the west have claimed it for years and so have we. When you saw Llyr, he had just returned from a parley. He's managed to secure agreement to settle the dispute once and for all, their champion against ours, in single combat."

Lucius guessed what was coming. "And I suppose he is to be your champion."

"Yes, he is. No one better to fight for land that is rightfully ours."

No one better to get his head lopped off.

"You don't seem very interested."

"I'm not. Your squabbles are nothing to me."

"But they should be. They should be."

"Why should they be?"

"Because you, Lucius Matius, are part of the prize."

In the late afternoon the sun hung low in the sky, blood red and baleful. Low murmurs of anticipation rippled through the crowd of Silures, gathered in a circle on the disputed land. Lucius stood next to Aneirin, for once not the center of attention.

A swelling murmur from the crowd drew his attention away from Hafod, who was waiting in silence, staring at his feet.

Llyr walked into the ring. His hair was stiff with some whitish paste and stood out from his head in spiked hackles of aggression. From the torc at his throat to his ankles, his naked body was painted blue, the cursive lines and elaborate knots following the curvature of muscle. A single stripe swept across his nose, from cheekbone to cheekbone, and his eyelids were darkened. His cock hung defenseless from a tight groin as he waited, grim-faced, testing the edge of his blade with his thumb. In his grave absorption, he had the stillness of every warrior who contemplates death, and in his stillness, he was beautiful.

"We keep to the old ways," Aneirin remarked. "Sword, shield and a man's own strength."

"Will they fight to the death?"

"If the loser fights well, he'll be given the honor of a quick death. If not, he'll be allowed to live out his life in shame. Pray to your gods that Llyr wins. Your balls depend on it."

"What do you mean?"

"Didn't I mention it? We keep our slaves entire." He nodded at a section of the crowd. "*They* castrate."

Lucius stared at the old man, his bowels turning to water.

"Look, there's Amren. A good fighter, but Llyr should best him."

The two combatants raised their swords in a brief salute and the crowd fell silent. Slowly they circled, testing the ground, finding their balance, each trying to maneuver the other into the sun. Amren made the first vicious lunge—thrown off by Llyr's nonchalant, shield. They withdrew, and the patient padding resumed, feet seeking purchase on the treacherous grass. Llyr leaped into the attack, steel clanging furiously on steel, blade slicing the air in the deadly dance, driving his opponent back. Amren recovered, and Llyr met him in a bone-jarring clash as they strained, face to grimacing face, blade to guard. They sprang apart, chests heaving and fists tightening on slippery grips. Amren lashed out his foot and caught Llyr on the thigh, following with a volley of kicks. The air between them grew thick with the snarls of fighting dogs, hungry for flesh. Shields up, sweat flying, they swung and slashed and stabbed in a ringing clamor of steel, neither giving, neither gaining until, exhausted, Llyr lowered his shield and his trembling sword arm dropped. Amren instantly sprang, but too wildly and off balance. Llyr whipped back, spun and crashed his shield into the man's face, almost knocking him off his feet. He came forward then, and with each step he punched the pommel of his sword into the man's skull in a terrible rain of blows. Amren went down like a felled oak. Llyr walked up to him and placed the point of his sword against his throat. In the open-mouthed, eye-bulging hush that had fallen on the crowd, he spoke quietly over him. His shoulders bunched, and with all his strength behind it, he drove the blade home.

Night had fallen. In the lamplight, the intricate designs on the walls of Llyr's house seemed to writhe and coil, serpents devouring their own tails. The guard at the door shoved Lucius hard and he took a stumbling step forward.

Llyr was sitting on a high-backed chair, idly turning a knife over and over between his fingers as a woman rebraided his hair. He was bare to the waist, the blue woad and spatters of blood cleaned away. A mesh of tattoos covered his chest and upper arms down to the gold armlets above his elbows. Hafod was lounging on a bed of wolf skins, teasing a hound by offering a bone, then jerking it away from the slavering chops.

"Sit," said Llyr, indicating a bench. The woman murmured something under her breath that made him smile, and then continued her work, deftly weaving gold beads into the ends of the plaits. "Roman, you called me a barbarian. Is that truly what you think we are?"

Lucius followed the knife as the prince shaved it over the hair on his forearm. "Yes."

Hafod uncurled. "Honest, but no less an insult."

"Hafod speaks the lingua Latina, but as you hear, his accent is worse than mine." Llyr ducked, grinning, as the bone flew through the air and the hound skittered after it. "Tell me," he continued, "how long have you been captive here?"

His eyes still on the knife, and the hairs trickling from the blade, Lucius said, "Five days."

"And in that time, have you seen slaves scourged until the bone breaks through the skin of their backs? Or a man pitted against a wild beast? Have you seen a line of crosses hung with suffocating bodies? No, I thought not." He laid the knife down. "A legionary has no wife, I know, but do you have a mother? Sisters?"

"Both."

"Are they full citizens of Rome?"

Despite his fear, Lucius smiled. "Citizens? *Women?*"

"See how we differ? Our women are free under our laws, equal to any man." He gestured to the woman, who came to stand at his side. "This is Rhiannedd. She orders her own life, does what she wants, chooses who she wants." He widened dark eyes. "And who she chooses now, legionary, is you."

The woman looked Lucius up and down, a faint smile on her face. When, shifting uneasily on the bench, he said nothing, she reached a hand to the enameled brooch at her shoulder and pulled out the pin. The cloth fell away, revealing heavy breasts, tipped with generous nipples.

Llyr stroked her thigh. "Beautiful, aren't they? Those tips... like sweet, dark berries. Rhiannedd is a delightful bedmate, or so I'm told. You'd like to lie with her, wouldn't you?"

A week after Lucius took on the toga of a man, his cousin had bought him a prostitute from the arches under the circus, a soft-bodied, honey-skinned Syrian with lips like ripe figs. He had taken her eagerly enough, curious about the mysterious crevices and folds between her legs, but, curiosity and cock satisfied, he'd had no wish to see them again. Or touch any more wet pinkness with his fingers, let alone sink his cock into it. He dropped his eyes from the creamy breasts.

"No," Llyr murmured, "it's a different kind of tip you want to feel growing hard on your tongue, isn't it?" He gave her rump a friendly slap to help her on her way, and she pouted and sauntered past Lucius, knocking knuckles on his head as she went, the hound with her.

From behind, Hafod slid his hands around Llyr's neck and Llyr took one and brought it to his mouth to nuzzle the palm. "I intend to free you, Lucius Matius Dexion. Are you surprised— ah, Hafod..." He broke off to lift his face to his lover, and Lucius again watched them kiss, a deep, languorous kiss behind the concealing fall of Hafod's braids. Llyr bent his arm up to cup Hafod's cheek, the armlet tight around the pale bulge of muscle. *Two men*, Lucius thought—*yes, this is how it should be. Male with male, cock responding to cock, each growing hard, so hard from the kiss.* His own jolted, hot squirms thrilled through the shaft, and he felt his mouth grow dry with lust.

Llyr caught Hafod's wrists and held them crossed on his chest. "You're free to go, Lucius. Return to your garrison and tell the men of Isca the truth of what you found here. Tell them how the barbarian prince treated his captive. Tell them that you weren't treated like a slave or a pack animal." He tilted his head. "What's this? I don't see you leaping to your feet and racing for the door. Is there something that's keeping your cold Roman heart here?"

"Or your hard Roman cock," Hafod added, mouthing Llyr's ear.

"We fight for our land and we slaughter our enemies, just as you do. But we don't rape, Lucius. If a man wants the taste of a barbarian mouth or the pleasure of a barbarian prick, he only has to ask. It's a courtesy we show our guests, do you see?" He smiled lazily and spread his legs and fingered the stag's head buckle on his belt. "You can leave now, empty, or go at dawn, full of barbarian seed."

The offer rang in the shadows. He was free. Free to return to his comrades, to yell the password to the drawn swords at the garrison gate. He looked at the door and then back to the men. Their hands were on each other, but their eyes were on him.

"Dawn," he said.

"Do you have a lover?" Llyr asked, blowing on his chest.

Lucius shifted on the rough wolf skin, wanting those warm lips to kiss his nipples the way they'd kissed his mouth. "There is a man I love."

"Mmm, not the same thing at all. And what do you do

together, you and this man? Does he give you what you want? Does he satisfy you?"

"No...not in the way I want him to. But that way...it's shameful for a man to play the woman's part."

Llyr leaned his head on his hand, watching intently as Hafod at last lowered his head to suckle the desperate nipple, sending sharp surges of pleasure pulsing to Lucius's cock. "How strange you Romans are! How can there be a *woman's* part when two men love? When fine warriors unite, they glorify their manhood and each other. This man of yours, he withheld himself from you? He refused you?"

"Did he refuse you this?" Hafod asked. He kissed the snaking ridge of muscle above Lucius's hip, then opened his mouth and swallowed his shaft to the root.

The guards outside heard it. The revelers reeling drunkenly from Llyr's victory feast heard it. The night watch in Isca might have heard the cry of agonized joy that tore from his throat. Nothing, nothing had felt as wonderful to him as Hafod's mouth. Unless it was Llyr's hand caressing his balls.

"Hafod's good at that, isn't he? Open your legs...bring them up. Let him...yes, that's it. He loves to do that."

"And *he* loves to watch." Hafod held Lucius's buttocks apart, strong fingers at the rim of his hole, waiting until Llyr had moved farther down the bed, and could see what he was doing. His tongue swept in languid laps, around and around the cramping flesh, darting and probing inward as he sucked. Lucius moaned in a daze of pleasure as Hafod wet his finger and slid it into him. In and out, stretching the thick ring, in and out, working it loose. Each thrust, each curl of the finger against the soft walls of his gut lifted his cock and forced another bead of clear seed to drip to his belly. But when he began to pant and rock his hips, Hafod eased his finger out.

The bitter scent of rosemary rose from the jar that Llyr held and grew stronger when the prince scooped out a little and rubbed it between finger and thumb. *Very good for easing and loosening.*

"Give or take?" he asked Lucius.

"Give or take?" Hafod repeated. "At least, to begin with."

"Please, Marcellus."

"No. Never. Be content with this." Marcellus tightened his arms around Lucius's chest and kissed the back of his neck. His cock slid, thrusting steadily between Lucius's thighs.

"I want you to. Please—" He lowered his ass, trying to get the shaft to his hole, but Marcellus pressed his heavy weight onto Lucius's back, pinning him.

"Make you less of a man? Ruin my darling? No, Lucius, this is enough, this is good—"

And though he wanted to weep at the dreary waste of it, he lay and let Marcellus plunge through his legs and handle his cock until their seed spurted, wetting the sheet.

"Take."

"Good," Llyr said, lying on his side. "I want to take this time, too." He raised his thigh and held his knee in the crook of his elbow.

Hafod smiled at Lucius's puzzled frown. "You in him, Lucius, and I in you. I'm better shaped for a virgin." It was true. Hafod's cock was arrow-headed, narrowing at the crown, whereas Llyr swelled. He took the rosemary jar and painted Lucius's prick with a thick coat of the oily salve. "And him, now. Prepare him."

The cleft between Llyr's buttocks was dense with hair, and Lucius wondered whether he would ever find the hole. But there it was, the little dip. It opened easily and seemed to suck his fingers in. So strange, so wonderful, the smooth inside of a man. The prince tossed his handsome head and moaned and stroked himself.

"Good," Hafod growled, and settled behind him. "Now."

Lucius fitted his hips to the waiting ass. Unpracticed as he was, he knew enough to enter with care, but the little mouth had yawned widely and swallowed his shaft in one long glide. A river of fire raced through his veins, the pleasure so intense that he hardly felt Hafod's wet cock nudging his own hole or heard his hoarse commands.

"Don't fight me, Roman. Let me in. Ssh, ssh...yes, that's it, that's it. Gently now, gently now, feel me...yes...*aah*!"

Back to chest, back to sweating chest, the three locked. Llyr reached his hand to Lucius's trembling flank and Hafod covered it, linking their fingers.

"Am I hurting you?" he murmured, kissing Lucius's neck.

He felt as if his entrails had been opened with a blade, but the pain was sweet, as welcome as the pleasure. "No."

"Move then. Hold him and move in him."

Lucius took hold of Llyr's prick and felt the rigid flesh quiver. He pressed into him until their balls met and felt Hafod's echoing thrust. They moved, and the scents of rosemary and sweat rose from their heated bodies, and the darker perfume, too, that came from their joining. Llyr gave a trailing groan when Lucius's cock slid over a swollen place inside him, and Hafod thrust savagely in response, as if answering a cry that he had heard many times before. Hearing it, Lucius's seed began to rise and seethe, and the men who held him sensed it. Hafod gripped his hip and drove into him, again and again, jolting his body and forcing him in turn deep into Llyr. The cock in his fist tightened and thick seed spurted, hot and abundant, just as his own flooded Llyr. Hafod howled and jerked and Lucius finally took what he had wanted for so long. It wasn't Marcellus who filled him, but a man's seed was a man's seed, and as he lay, and his heart slowed, and his lovers peeled their sticky skin away from his, it seeped into his scalded flesh, and he smiled.

"*Decanus.*"

Lucius turned on the threshold.

Llyr folded his arms behind his head and Hafod's sleepy hand crept over his belly to draw him close. "Enemies took pleasure together and, yes, it was good. But enemies we remain. If we meet again, if I ever encounter you on my land again, I'll kill you."

Lucius stared and bowed his head in acknowledgment of the somber words. He pushed through the door and lifted his face to the soft dawn of Cambria.

DRAGON'S SON

Evey Brett

"You should have been here sooner," Shirou told me as I arrived at his father's room, short of breath and limping worse than usual after tripping over bodies in the courtyard and climbing two flights of stairs. The attack on Hoshi Castle had come before dawn, finding us ill prepared. The castle, hastily built as Lord Ryunosuke's last defense, was sheltered by the mountain on three sides. Unfortunately, that same protection also left us vulnerable to siege.

"I came as quickly as I could, Shirou-san. I was tending to the wounded." A number of my assistants and the able-bodied were caring for the injured as well as they could, but the losses were going to be high.

"My father needs you more." Shirou was acting impatiently to cover his unease. I knew those pout lines well; he'd worn them even when we were children.

He slid open the door and I ducked inside into a stifling but well-lit room. A mural featuring a golden dragon fighting a tiger adorned the far wall, the savagery of the entwined creatures reminiscent of Lord Ryunosuke's feats in battle. The image was meant to symbolize duality and balance between opposing forces, but it was the daimyo's constant hardness and refusal to yield that had left him lying on a pallet, a pale shadow of what he once had been.

"The physician has come, Father," Shirou said, kneeling on one side while I knelt painfully on the other. The incense wafting through the room did little to cover the stink of battle and blood.

There was no answer save for hoarse, ragged breaths. The daimyo's armor had been carefully peeled away, leaving him in his bloodstained kimono. There was a gaping slice across his belly and another in his thigh, but the cleanest—and worst— was the arrow that had lodged in his chest. I hardly needed to lift the bandage to know what I would find.

I exchanged a glance with Shirou. There were no words needed. He knew a mortal wound as well as I. "It's too soon," he said, looking away.

Lord Ryunosuke's eyes fluttered open. His gaze fixed on his son and waited until Shirou had the courage to look back. The daimyo's voice was nearly too soft to hear. "It's her fault."

Shirou's face hardened. Behind that mask of stone, I sensed his building anger.

"Help me." Lord Ryunosuke's hand weakly lifted.

Shirou shuddered, but, being the obedient son he was, bowed and curled the daimyo's fingers around the shaft. He left his hand atop his father's. "Swift journeys, Father," he said.

One swift yank, and it was over in moments. Shirou dropped the arrow as if it were poisoned. At his gesture, a priest and numerous servants rushed in. Several cried out and moaned, the start of ritual mourning, but Shirou's face was taut and unchanged. He remained stalwart as he bent over and accompanied the priest in offering final prayers.

"There is work to be done," he said before stalking out.

I saw little of him throughout the afternoon and evening

as he accepted condolences and doled out the various honors due to his warriors whenever they brought him the head of an enemy. There weren't many of the latter, though Shirou had taken a number of his own. Because the Katamura clan had used a number of firearms while we'd been forced to employ archers, the battle had cost us more than half of our men while our rivals had lost only a few dozen of theirs. The wounds were deadlier and more gruesome, not to mention difficult to deal with.

It wasn't until nightfall, when a messenger fetched me to Shirou's room, that I was able to speak with him again. I knelt and bowed low to my new lord and commander. "Shirou-sama?"

He shook his head wearily. "Don't. I can't stand it. Not from you."

I waited, shifting just enough to ease the ache in my bad leg. We were all exhausted, but he was pale and weary to the point that I worried. I didn't see any obvious wounds, but there could be others. I'd scolded him more than once for not telling me about severe blows he'd taken to his abdomen and kidneys.

His body servant helped him strip his armor, then fetched food, wine and a basin of clean water. Shirou said nothing, did nothing until the boy had returned with the requested items and again disappeared.

"Let me," I said, indicating the basin. At his nod, I wet the sponge and washed his face and neck. A drafty room at the top of a keep was a poor stand-in for the luxuriant baths we'd shared at his father's main castle, but it would do.

Without my urging, he shrugged off his kimono so that he was bare to the waist. Other than a few new bruises and scars, his lean, muscular body was the same one I'd known. I ran my hands along his head, neck, shoulders and arms, feeling tension but no heat that might indicate injury. He gave a little sigh as I swept his long ebony hair aside and sponged his back, cleansing the remnants of the day's battle from his skin.

Much as I loved being near him once more, it pained me

as well. My beautiful, bright-eyed Shirou was gone, replaced by a man old before his time. I longed to kiss him between the shoulder blades and do what I could to ease his anguished mind, but I feared adding to his grief.

When I was done and had helped him dress in a clean kimono, he poured a cup of sake for each of us and drank. "Tomorrow, I will take my father's place. I will be the daimyo in his stead." He spoke matter-of-factly, yet I knew him too well to miss the trembling in his hands.

"I'm sorry." Commanding an army and fighting wars to defend or increase his clan's holdings was the last thing Shirou wanted, and for many years it seemed he might escape his fate. As his father's fourth son, he'd been considered extraneous and allowed to take refuge in a mountain temple, only to be recalled when his first brother died in battle, the second of fever and the third by poison. He was as much a warrior as any of his brothers, having been trained as a swordsman from the time he was old enough to hold a practice blade, but simply shared my preference to travel the road of peace.

I was the third son of a samurai who lived on the daimyo's estate, and a childhood accident with a horse had left me with a crippled leg and no hope of following my father's profession. While I healed, my father was wise enough to nurture my scientific interest and arranged for me to share Shirou's tutor. Shirou and I had become fast friends, though when both of us had come of age, I'd been sent to learn from the best physicians and he'd gone to the mountains. Neither of us expected to see the other again, and it was a cruel fate indeed that had brought us together under such bloody circumstances.

"And I will have to wear *that*." He nodded at the corner of the tent where a servant had set the newly cleaned and repaired armor on a stand. It was a beautiful piece of art, the panels lacquered a deep maroon and lined with gold. The breastplate had been carved and painted with golden triangles representing dragon scales, the symbol of his house. The swords, both in matching scabbards, rested on their own rack.

He reached out to stroke the armor, but before he could, a shudder racked his body. He leaped to his feet and dashed out of the room before I could catch him.

I grabbed my kit and hurried into the hallway, noting the startled faces of his servants and followers. "Stay here. I'll see to him," I said, cursing my inability to travel swiftly.

On instinct, I headed toward the stables and sighted a knot of stable hands and guards outside the door, all looking rather morose. They'd obviously been ordered to leave their posts. "Get some food and find a place to sleep. Don't bother us unless I call for you," I told them. They bowed and scattered. I may not have been a warrior, but I had status enough to be obeyed.

Inside, the scent of sweet hay, oats and damp horse welcomed my nose. Several horses perked up at my approach, and my favorite mount, a quiet gray mare, whickered. I spared her a scratch between the ears before I found Shirou bent over a trough, scrubbing his bare hands in the water. The blood had long since been washed away, yet he kept at it, scraping hard enough to tear his skin.

"Enough," I said, taking Shirou's hands in my own. They were frigid. I wrapped my arms around him and he shivered. A kiss to his cheek and he trembled uncontrollably. Shirou had fought in a battle this morning, but a greater war raged in his heart. When he met my gaze, I saw he had indeed been hurt, but the evidence wasn't on his flesh; it was in his eyes.

I led him into the section housing tack and blankets, including Lord Ryunosuke's worked saddle draped with the tiger skin rug he'd used for a pad. He'd gotten the pelt on a mission to China when he'd hunted and killed the beast himself.

We sank to the ground amidst the comforting scents of leather and horse. I stretched out my bad leg and had the stone wall for support while Shirou sat between my thighs and leaned against me like a worn-out child. In here, alone, the formalities of rank dropped, and we became the two boys we had been, finding comfort in the other's presence. For months after my accident, I'd woken in terrible pain, and Shirou had held me, talking me through the worst of it. After such devoted care, I'd sworn to serve his family and, by default, him, but he never used his rank to abuse me. Quite the opposite.

Shirou fingered the tiger skin. "It's my father's fault we're doing battle with the Katamura clan. All because of a woman."

As the tale went, Lord Ryunosuke had courted one of the Katamura daughters back when they'd been our allies. As the Katamura told it, Lord Ryunosuke had made improper advances. From Lord Ryunosuke's perspective, it was the daughter who had made an unforgivable slight toward him. Both clans insisted they were telling the truth, and since no agreement could be reached, they'd gone to war to settle their dispute.

"The Katamura want my clan dead. Perhaps I should save them the trouble of hunting me down and send you to them with my head."

A chill pooled in my belly. I'd spent time in the teahouses with both men and women, but Shirou was the one I loved, and I could not bear the thought of losing him to his own hand or any other. "No."

He twisted around to face me. "Why not?"

Words clogged my throat. So instead of answering, I kissed him.

I felt him tense, and momentarily wondered if I'd acted wrongly, but then he relaxed and met my questing tongue with his. He tasted of sake and had the same heady effect on my thoughts.

The stable was pleasantly warm, yet I shivered when Shirou pulled my obi loose so that my kimono fell open. With a shrug, the silk garment dropped and pooled around my waist. Shirou stroked my back, pausing when he reached a particularly sore spot caused by the strain of my crooked walk. With a mischievous look in his eye, he draped the tiger skin on the ground. "Lie down," he said, and, since he was my commander, I obeyed, stretching out on the soft pelt. "Do you have any oils?"

"In the box," I told him.

More agile than I, Shirou grabbed my surgeon's kit and sorted through the contents until he found a bottle I knew he was familiar with. He poured a few drops of oil on his hands and dug firmly into my aching flesh. My bad leg was twisted and shriveled compared to the other, and Shirou took extra care in handling it. Much of his skill he'd learned in the dojo, but I'd taught him a few things after I'd advanced in my studies. "I don't know how you do it," he said, "living each day in such pain but continuing on."

I groaned as he pressed a tender point. "We both do what we must."

He was silent a while, and I focused on his strong, expert fingers. The fragrant oil soon warmed me as it became apparent that he was using me both as a distraction and as a means of working out his frustrations. I minded neither as long as I was being of use to him; his mind worked best when his body was kept busy.

"What am I going to do, Kenji? We don't have the men or weapons to win a battle. If we do nothing, we will starve within the month. There is no one to come to our aid. My father drove away all of his allies. His sister passed of fever and cannot act as witness."

He wasn't really asking me. He had advisors, generals and any number of others capable of giving a more expert opinion; Lord Ryunosuke's staff was more than eager to offer their advice and probably had been all day. His hands grew firmer, harder, as his vexation came to the fore, resulting in soreness both agonizing and pleasant. "He left you in an impossible position."

"More than impossible." He rolled me over so that I lay

looking up at him. Twenty-five years old, Shirou had lost none of his youthful beauty. His hair, freed of its usual topknot, flowed around his shoulders. "If he hadn't died, he would have sent his men on a final strike. We all would have perished. There is no honor in loyalty to a man determined to destroy himself as well as his men."

"He's dead. His men are yours. How will you lead them?"

Another few drops of oil and he touched me again, sliding his hands across my chest and shoulders. The friction warmed me to the point that I felt feverish. I closed my eyes as Shirou continued to work, massaging my belly—empty except for sake, since I'd had no time to eat—then my legs.

So relaxed was I that I didn't realize for some time that he'd stopped. I became aware of his presence and heat radiating from his body. Opening my eyes, I saw his face hovering above mine.

"Kenji." His voice was low and hoarse with need, which caused a rush of tingling below my belly. My cock stiffened within my loin wrap, but I had no chance to free it before Shirou straddled me and bent down. His lips met mine and we kissed, tongues meeting, his driving deeply into my mouth. I moaned at the pleasure of having him against me at last.

Lying on the pelt, I couldn't help but be reminded of the dragon and tiger mural in the late daimyo's room. For all that the joining of dragon and tiger represented balance, I'd always seen it as an image of war, one clan fighting another for dominance. Lord Ryunosuke, known as the Golden Dragon, had ridden into battle on his tiger skin rug, another vicious blending of the two creatures.

But as Shirou tangled his limbs around mine, I saw the mural differently. In the arms of the Golden Dragon's son, I could imagine those sinuously entwined creatures fighting a battle not of war but of lust.

Whether it was the tiger's spirit or Lord Ryunosuke's, my blood burned with the thrill of battles I'd witnessed but never been able to fight in. I grabbed at Shirou, tearing at his kimono and loin wrap until he was naked, every part of him available for me to touch. He did the same, untying my loin wrap and tossing it aside so that my craving for him was made obvious by my jutting cock. The usual aches of my body faded, replaced by an intense, hot-blooded need.

I dug into his flesh, nipping at his neck and lapping the salt. He responded with a low moan and pressed himself against me so that our cocks met and rubbed against each other, increasing our frenzy.

The oil had left my skin slick. He slipped against me and laughed, reminding me of when we'd been inexperienced, fumbling boys, giggling to hide our nervousness and our intense desire for each other. As we'd grown into men, the attraction had deepened into full-fledged ardor that nothing, not women, not even separation and our later involvement in war could shake.

Perhaps it was obscene to couple on one of his father's prized possessions, but we were too far gone to care. He pinned me down and kissed me. I was helpless as he held me down and grabbed my cock, hands firm and efficient as they glided up and down my shaft. When I was near to bursting, he rolled me onto my side, so that no weight rested on my bad leg, and arranged me to provide him with the best access from the rear.

He was always gentle, my Shirou. The clove oil was ready in his hands, and he prepared me well, sliding his fingers between my buttocks and then inside me. His tender explorations caused me to squirm when he pressed against certain points. I shuddered as the pressure deep within me built.

Then he positioned himself so that his hardness nudged my backside. His entry was swift and sure, robbing me of my breath as he filled me. He went slowly at first, letting me become used to his presence, then angled his hips to penetrate me even more deeply.

Flesh slapped against flesh as he picked up speed. I lay there, mouth wide and panting. I think it pleased him to have this chance to be gentle and soft when so much of his life dealt with the discipline and harshness of warfare.

I tensed, sensing impending climax. He grasped me, holding tightly as he thrust one last time. The hot rush of his seed burst within me. Moments later, I joined him, groaning in mixed bliss and relief at so great a release.

He flopped onto his back, gasping. I rolled over and stroked his sweaty chest. "Let them take the castle. We can fake your suicide. You can go back to the temple and live in peace."

"And escape how?" he asked. "Over the mountain? That's the only way out of here, and you couldn't manage it." He took my hand in his and kissed it. "I won't leave you to die alone."

I clung to him, all too aware of his despair. There was nothing I wouldn't do for my Shirou, no act I wouldn't perform to save him from death or dishonor.

When he fell asleep—which didn't take long, exhausted as he was—I silently dressed and hobbled upstairs. I gestured to two of the guards keeping watch outside Lord Ryunosuke's room and said, "If you wish to save your master's life, help me."

Not long after, I was in Shirou's armor and astride his handsome black gelding heading down the road toward the Katamura encampment. The sun was just rising over the distant hills when a half dozen guards surrounded me.

Doing my best to imitate Shirou's voice and manner, I said, "I am Masaka Shirou. My father, Masaka Ryunosuke, is dead." I removed the bundle tied to the saddle and tossed it to the nearest guard. "Take that to your master. Tell him I wish to negotiate a treaty."

The guard dashed inside. It wasn't long before he returned and gestured frantically for me to follow. I stayed mounted as long as I could and prayed they would take my shuffling walk for a recent injury.

Just outside the curtained area that served as the daimyo's meeting place, I eased off the horse and limped inside. The daimyo, Katamura Shingen, was an old man, nearly seventy, but sat atop his folding stool with energy and intelligence. Two of his sons sat nearby, discouraging any thought of attack, even if that had been my plan. All watched me with ill-concealed dislike as I entered and prostrated myself, trying not to wince at the pain shooting through my leg and hip. Lord Ryunosuke's head sat unwrapped at the elder Katamura's feet, the eyes staring emptily at the lightening sky.

"What do you want, Masaka?" asked Katamura.

"I offer my life in exchange for a treaty. End this battle between our two people. My father is dead. Enough blood has been shed." To prove my sincerity, I laid Shirou's short sword just in front of me. "I am at your mercy, Great Lord."

Further discussion was interrupted by the patter of footsteps. The flap was pulled aside and another man hurried forward and bowed low. I dared not look over to see who it was.

"What is this?" Katamura asked angrily.

The man next to me spoke, and somehow I wasn't surprised to find it was Shirou. "I am the true son of Masaka Ryunosuke. This man is my physician. An imposter."

My heart sank. We were both going to die in shame.

"Sit up," Katamura demanded.

I did. A guard yanked off my helmet, then unfastened the armor. Once it was gone, my thinner form made it apparent which of us was the warrior and which was not. The daimyo looked from me to Shirou and back again. "Your name, physician?"

I bowed. "Yoshida Kenji, Great Lord."

"Yoshida Kenji, son of the samurai Yoshida Noribu, the Tiger of Eisai?"

It had been some time since I'd heard my father's nickname, which he'd gained by his fierceness in battle and the number of heads he'd brought back. "The same, Great Lord."

Katamura looked thoughtful a moment, then asked, "You are willing to die for your master. What makes him so worthy of your loyalty?"

"We have been sworn friends since childhood. I have vowed to aid him even at the expense of my own life. He spent time in a temple before being recalled to his father's side. It is my greatest wish that he return there and live the life of peace he craves. When we were boys, we spoke of saving lives, not ending them. This is not my lord's fight but his father's, and I would see it ended."

Shirou made a choked sound. Katamura turned his attention to him. "And you, dragon's son. This man falsely represented you and claimed to represent your intentions. What do you think his punishment should be?"

"He should die for his actions." The words came out hard.

"But you have misgivings."

Shirou's voice trembled. "He is my strength when I have none. Without him, I will fall. If you wish one of us to die, I beg for your mercy to kill us both."

"And if I ask you to kill him first?"

"Then I will do so." From the corner of my eye I saw Shirou rise and move into the proper stance. His katana hissed as he removed it from its sheath. Heart hammering, I prostrated myself, neck exposed, and waited for the final blow.

Time seemed to stop. My senses intensified. I felt the blood rushing through my veins and cool air brush my cheeks and neck. Curtains rustled. Somewhere beyond, an impatient horse raked the earth with its hoof. Sharp daggers of pain shot through my leg, so intense I wanted to weep with the relief of knowing it would end soon.

Even without looking, I sensed Shirou's anger that I'd left him and made it look as though he were too cowardly to come himself. My hope rested in him knowing I'd done it out of love for him. Our coupling had brought us so close that in our final moments we were in accord. If one of us died, the other would commit suicide. Nothing would separate us.

"If I let you live," Katamura said, "what are your intentions?"

Shirou didn't move. "I am the last of the dragon's line. I have no interest in his castles, his lands or his holdings. I would lay down my sword, retreat to the mountains and live the remainder of my life as a monk."

"He lies," said one of the sons. "It's a trick. He will have laid traps and men all over the castle."

"I swear to you, I have not," Shirou replied calmly. "My father's property and all that is in it is yours. You may have what men choose to declare their loyalty to you. I will put my name to whatever paper you care to prepare."

"Do you care nothing for your father's honor?" asked the other son.

"My father tarnished his name as soon as he spread lies about your honored sister and put his own pride first."

This took the Katamura aback. There was a collective inhale and a few quiet mutters. "Do you know this to be the truth?" Katamura asked.

Shirou lowered the sword. He held it at his side as if it were too heavy to lift. "There must be balance in power. My father was more tiger than dragon, despite his name. He was a hard man who knew nothing of softness. Even on his deathbed, he refused to admit he'd been in the wrong. I ask that the Great Lord be merciful and allow me to provide the balance by yielding honorably to his greater strength."

I held my breath, well aware Katamura was within his rights to slay us both and put a final, permanent end to the war. I was still ready and willing to die, but I grieved that Shirou might make such a plea in vain.

"So be it. I accept your terms." Katamura spoke to a servant who presented Shirou with paper, ink and brush. He took his time, writing each word carefully and clearly. When he was done, he handed it to the servant who passed it to Katamura.

The daimyo looked the paper over, then nodded approvingly. "Go," he commanded, gesturing imperially. "Take your horses. You have two days to reach the temple. Should either of you leave it again, your lives are forfeit."

I could barely stand after maintaining one position for so long, but Shirou helped me to my feet. This time, he was my strength, for I could not have mounted without his help. As soon as he climbed aboard his father's white stallion, we raced out of the encampment and left our pasts behind.

The next two days were a blur of worry and pain. Shirou pressed hard, determined to get me to safety. I clung doggedly to the saddle, unwilling to let my discomfort slow us down and risk our lives. We had neither rations nor weapons, having left the latter behind as a sign of good faith, so by the time we reached the temple, we were weary and starved.

The monks made us welcome. Shirou was already known to them, and I had little fear of finding my own place as they were eager to have another healer among them. At Shirou's request, we had a room to ourselves. The fine horses and tack would be sold to benefit the temple, and while personal possessions were discouraged, Shirou had made one notable exception.

I lay on it, reveling in the soft, striped fur against my bare skin while Shirou tended to my painful leg. A bath in the hot springs had helped, but it was no replacement for Shirou's attentions.

With oiled hands, he worked up my thighs to the parts in between. I arched back and he took advantage of the increased access by thrusting his hand beneath my balls and stroking until my cock was achingly hard.

Then, supporting my bad leg, he raised my hips and speared

me. Pain blossomed for an instant before changing to a profound, aching pleasure that spread through my belly. Our gazes locked and held. Master and servant. Warrior and healer. I was his support and he was mine, and it was never so fulfilling as now, when we were joined together and aiding each other in reaching mutual pleasure.

Climax rose and erupted, leaving us both tired and twitching in the aftermath. I rested my head and shoulder on his chest, listening to the fierce beat of his heart. "Dragon's son."

He laid a sweet kiss upon my forehead. "Tiger's son."

We curled together, tiger and dragon, in perfect balance.

TO THE VICTOR

Salome Wilde

His entrance was so warm and welcoming that I feared I would spill my seed before I'd even begun to claim my prize. The moon shone over his exposed flesh, and I reveled in the vision of his firm ass and muscled thighs. I gritted my teeth and fought for self-control as he urged me on with low grunts and arched his massive back to meet my every thrust. All but the pleasure of our bodies united as one fled from my mind, even the risk that we might be caught, out in the open of the village square in the late hours of a cold night.

But I hasten too quickly toward my tale's conclusion. Let me begin again...

The defeat of the tyrant Valushkin should have been my greatest triumph. His downfall was deemed impossible by all but fools and perhaps those few of my intimate acquaintance who knew the bottomless depth of my determination. His army was the mightiest ever assembled in our lands, governed by his indomitable will, his prowess as a leader and the ferocity of his troops. From such power came Valushkin's iron rule over the kingdom, reflected in a vast, towering castle that overlooked villages and farms populated by a cowed peasantry.

I knew this world intimately, witnessed the warlord's methods firsthand. As the bastard son of a lowly palace guard and a village whore, I was raised in the dirt and quickly learned to steal and cheat, knowing nothing would be given to me in this life unless I took it for myself. I grew to quiet strength and more than average intelligence in the shadow of Valushkin's ruthless magnificence. Had I brawn but little brain, I would no doubt have made a meager existence as a blacksmith's apprentice or a conscripted soldier, to have my blood spilled in my first taste of battle. But fate turned otherwise.

My keen and ambitious mind first led me to the forest, where I joined a band of local rebels. I eagerly accepted the role of errand boy, lookout and bed warmer. Passed from man to man, I learned fighting and stealth by day and honest lust by night. Within a few short years, as I grew to rough-hewn manhood, I earned the trust of my fellows and increased our numbers. My skills in strategy and a taste for combat were matched only by my generous sexual appetites. Soon, the men made me their leader, and we began together the daunting efforts of building an army strong enough to defeat Valushkin.

Knowing our numbers insufficient, I advised that we turn to the warring steppe tribes. In time, and utilizing my glib tongue and swift sword, I brought them to our shared cause against the common enemy. Together, we swept in upon Valushkin's men on half a dozen fronts, shooting a thousand arrows from horseback at every pass. Before long, we had Valushkin's army in confusion and disarray. Defeat came at the steps of his very castle, where I challenged him to single combat. Heart racing and blood surging, we fought. Wills and blades of equal might clashed. After an exhausting and bloody hour, the generous fates favored me. I could scarcely believe that I'd bested him, and that my efforts had succeeded against all odds. Yet, it somehow also seemed inevitable. To wild cheers and howling cries, I held my bloody sword aloft in triumph as Valushkin was taken away in chains.

Some of the tyrant's forces fled. A few surrendered. Many, however, joined me, eager to serve a less tyrannical master. These men helped us to open the castle coffers and food stores to share all with the peasants who had been kept in poverty and mindless submission for too long. Wrongly held prisoners were released and slaves were freed. My name was heralded, and I gloried in it. My army and I had faced the greatest of challenges and won. I could not have known then that, for me, the true contest had yet to begin.

Valushkin, meanwhile, was put on public display, bound in heavy chain and staked to a post in the village square. The great and hated warlord would spend his final hours among the people whose lives he had held in his cold, merciless hands. They could watch as he froze to death or died of dehydration, left thereafter as food for the ravens.

Thoughts of this slow, ignominious death at first filled me with pleasure, drunk as I was with power. I gorged myself on food and flesh like the hero I was, and slept like a babe. On the third night, however, I found I could not rest. I was agitated and discontented, and therefore attempted to distract myself with the body of a wild, tattooed tribesman whose name I could not pronounce, then strove to drink myself into unconsciousness. My efforts, however, failed. I told myself I was merely anxious at the likelihood of dreams filled with images of death, of the slaughter of the many men who had died in my service. The truth, though, was far more selfish and more terrible. For I dreaded facing a sleeping echo of the moment Valushkin had met me at the palace gates, when I had finally faced him and beheld his enthralling, savage allure.

There was such frozen fierceness in those narrow, ice-blue eyes. A barbaric perfection burned in his bronzed, weather-beaten complexion. I marveled at the curl of his lip within his bearded jaw, his visage surrounded by a wild mane of blue-black hair. He wore no crown, but needed none to manifest his might. Then came his low, snarled consent to combat: the voice of a beautiful and dangerous animal. Though I had defeated him with sword, I suddenly realized a new battle had begun—within me. Even as I relished the despot's downfall, I knew myself awed beyond redemption by the man.

In frustration, I cursed his name aloud and heard it ring from the rafters of the great hall, bringing a rousing cheer from the men around me, who misunderstood entirely the meaning behind my cry. I grew feverish, pacing the floor like a tiger as I faced this abhorrent, inescapable truth. Finally, I retreated to a private chamber, where I donned the garb of a common guard and threw a heavy fur across my shoulders. In this way, I managed to escape the castle without notice. I then mounted a sturdy horse not my own and raced toward the village square. The mount's thudding hoofbeats in the snow were drowned by the hammering of my heart as my breath made streaming clouds against the light of the crescent moon.

As I drew nearer, trepidation assailed me. Though all in the kingdom had been ordered that Valushkin remain unmolested, there was still the possibility that I would find him mutilated, sans toes or fingers taken for souvenirs, even castrated. I winced at the thought and hastened on.

At last, I reached my goal, to find Valushkin slumped against the stake. As I dismounted, a cold wind ripped through me. I shuddered, but the hulking form before me did not move. I wondered whether I was too late. Or perhaps he only slept. I approached him carefully, as I would an injured bear. When I was close enough to breathe in the scent of dried blood and a headier personal musk, his eyes suddenly opened and I was captured by the flash of his ice-and-steel gaze.

"Valushkin," I hissed.

He straightened his back, eyes locked on mine.

"Are you enjoying my hospitality?" I mocked.

He merely sneered.

"Answer me," I demanded.

I watched his chapped lips stretch into a derisive grin, his beard flecked with frost. My hands balled into fists in response and I brought my arm up to swing. The arrogant monster! But I stopped myself. The target was too easy. I was the victor, and we both knew it. I turned away, feeling foolish. What was I doing here? I hadn't come to gloat. And if I'd come only to see the face of my terrible, beautiful enemy once more, now I had done so. I longed for wine and the comfort of a roaring fire. I strode back toward my horse, stiff with pride.

Above the crunch of the snow, I heard Valushkin's laugh.

Spinning on my heel, I was certain I would strike the arrogant beast. Before I reached him, however, he spoke.

"I've been waiting for you," he announced, his voice the low rumble of thunder.

I was struck dumb by the words and the way his eyes lit as they held me once more in their power. How could I answer? I had betrayed my own weakness by seeking out my fallen enemy and taunting him purposelessly. Though I had not come for the reason he obviously suspected, there was no sensible explanation for my presence. I stood, mute and lost.

"I unlocked these chains the first night," Valushkin continued as he held up his freed hands. "One of the villagers—curse all their selfish, ignorant souls—was kind enough to throw a chicken bone at me."

"Then why—"

"Am I still here?" he concluded for me. "As I said, I've been waiting for you."

I swallowed hard as Valushkin untangled himself from the heavy lengths of iron and came to stand before me. He did not exactly tower over me, but somehow he looked as if he had grown even more massive since our battle. At the very least, he seemed not the slightest bit weaker for his three days without food, drink or furs against the cold. I would not have been surprised had he unsheathed a hidden dagger and slain me on the spot. But this was not his plan.

A heavy arm fell across my shoulders. "Come," he said with amusement, kicking links of chain out of his way and guiding me to sit beside him against the low stone wall that surrounded the stake. "Let us talk, man to man."

Despite myself, I felt a thrill at my core. I tried to muster outrage or simple resistance, but failed. And still I did not speak.

"It was good to defeat me, wasn't it, my young vanquisher?"

Certainly it was. The most important day of my life, in fact. And I could see in his countenance that his question was genuine. How many had he himself defeated with zeal, over many years? I stared at a silver scar across his brow, wondering how many more like it covered his body. "Yes," I exhaled, hearing the arousal in my own voice too clearly.

"Yet your desire for me confuses you."

I nodded, even as I was disconcerted by the way he so easily pulled the truth from me, like the removal of a sliver.

"Do not let it," he advised with a grin. "There are times to think and times to act. You took my power with one sword, and now you wish to take me bodily with another." His eyes glittered as he glanced at the hardness growing between my legs. "It is as simple as that."

"Simple," I echoed, both question and answer, and, before I could say more, my mighty nemesis took my broad face in his huge hands and kissed me with the force of an avalanche. I felt the calluses on his palms and the thickness of his beard against my own. His wind-cracked lips parted, giving way to a warm and generous tongue. I feasted. And when he pulled away, we were both breathless.

"There is one condition to my surrender," Valushkin huffed.

"Afterward, you must let me tell you a story."

Lust-addled, I agreed without understanding. Then I watched as the mountain of a man began to unfasten his leathers. It was exactly the sight I anticipated: hairy, muscular thighs and a thick thatch surrounding a huge, rigid shaft. My fingers itched to touch it, and Valushkin chuckled as I tentatively reached out.

"Go on," he encouraged, leaning over to release my own straining member into his mighty grip.

Together, we knelt in the cold, the stars our only witnesses as we stroked each other with single-minded resolve, gazes locked to feed on the desire reflected in the other's eyes.

"I've been too rarely touched by a worthy opponent," Valushkin muttered, his voice thick.

I groaned. "I have rarely desired an opponent so greatly."

At that, he withdrew himself from my grasp and bent before me to take my heavy meat into his mouth. Such an act was not an inclination I often gave way to, either in the giving or the receiving. But the sight of his shaggy head at my groin, accompanied by the warm wetness of his tongue, roused me further. Soon enough, I realized its purpose. With neither oil nor tallow available, Valushkin was providing what little lubrication he could for himself. Rugged and ruthless he might be, but it was his hole that would be plundered.

After a short time, he pulled off, and I held myself firmly while he turned onto his hands and knees, leathers at his ankles. It is no exaggeration to say that I had never beheld so enticing a view. And I was ready and willing to take advantage of it. As I knelt, parted his cheeks and spit generously, he craned his neck to glance back at me. Those penetrating eyes, narrowed with need, bored into me just as surely as I would bore into that waiting orifice.

"Take me," he commanded.

I thrust home. When I began to withdraw, my foe and lover responded by tightening his muscles against me, so I had to fight to claim him fully. Our union was little different from our combat, though less bloody and far more brief than I wanted. Though I longed to give him the best shafting he had ever taken, my desire overwhelmed my ambitions. After only moments of riding him hard and fast, I reached the precipice. Balls deep, fingers clutching his brawny backside, I sprayed my seed into him with unrivaled force.

Soon thereafter, I withdrew and sat back on my heels. Valushkin hiked his leathers and came to sit beside me. He reached for the fur that had fallen from my shoulders and wrapped us both within it. I breathed heavily, as did Valushkin. Placing a hand on his cock, I found him thick but soft. Glancing beside us where he had knelt, I saw the small pool of his own release and was pleased.

"Now," he said, roughly brushing my matted hair from my brow, "it is time I tell you the truth about the nature of victory."

I nodded blearily, relaxed despite the cold and our vulnerable position. Were I caught with Valushkin on all fours, I might have explained it away as my due—the spoils of war. But there would be no answer for sitting in my enemy's arms as he shared a bedtime story.

"Like you," he began, "I was born into poverty, deprived of opportunity by circumstance. Quick of mind and great of stature, I easily assembled a band of rebels that grew, along with my reputation, as I fought for control of other groups of resisters and outlaws. Eventually, we defeated the warlord's troops." He paused to rub his throat before taking a clump of snow from the little wall and dissolving it in his mouth with relish. I regretted not having brought my leather flask and followed suit.

He continued. "The structure of such a tale is common, you are no doubt aware, even as the details vary. In my case, the lord against whom I campaigned was haply both loathed and loathsome—having suffered some debilitating, disfiguring ailment given to him, it was said, by his foreign-born wife. I made use of his weakness by demanding single combat, and easily bested him."

I listened with astonishment. I had not known there were any similarities between Valushkin and me. I'd always been told he'd been a spoiled youth, willful and barbaric. I heard more than once that he had sold his soul for power to some unnamed demon, though I did not truly credit it. Before I could consider the parallels between us further, Valushkin went on in a different tone, a faraway glow now in his eyes.

"I was overjoyed to have won freedom for the land I loved. I vowed to be a beneficent ruler, just and fair. My army of rebels would stay strong and honorable, like the noble cause that had united us."

"Yes," I breathed, "just so." I felt my own heart and hopes laid bare in Valushkin's words.

He frowned and pulled away to face me, brow furrowed. "How long do you think it was before my own lieutenants became greedy and corrupt? How long until the villagers fell back into their petty squabbles? Until warrior tribes demanded a return to the lifestyle they knew, stealing crops and women as they had since time immemorial? How few years thereafter before new bands of rebels began to form in the woods, aiming to bring down the ruler that had become a despot to keep some semblance of peace in his kingdom?" He stroked my cheek, tenderly. "And how long before I faced a reflection of my younger self in you?"

I was shocked, outraged. This could not be true. It was some trickery, a calculated plot by a ruthless madman to wean both the strength from my body and the sureness from my mind. "You will not reclaim the throne, Valushkin!" I spat. I rose to my feet. "I swear my life upon it." My heart pounded in my chest and I cursed myself for not lacking wit enough to have a sword at my side.

Valushkin looked up at me and gave a hearty and derisive laugh. "You idiot," he replied with a snort. "I don't want to reclaim it!" Rising beside me, he added, "Keep the rotten kingdom, O Mighty Conqueror, and may it give you as much misery as it gave me!"

Once again, Valushkin reduced me to silence. I stood, frozen to the spot, my thoughts racing. What if all he said was true? I recalled the frequent brawls among the tribesmen and the callous talk of riches and privilege among my deputies. I quickly faced the truth that it would not be long before I was as hated as Valushkin himself.

Valushkin had turned and began walking from the square.

"Where are you going?" I called after him, as loudly as I dared.

He turned back. "To exile myself—unless you have means to kill me?"

"I could summon aid," I said, without conviction.

"So you could," he answered, and smiled. The brightness of his eyes and his strong, white teeth were a beacon.

"My horse can carry two," I offered.

"Indeed it can," he agreed.

So we rode, far into the night and as far as we could get from the civilized world of soured causes and heroic tyrants, to claim together the spoils of freedom.

CAPTIVES

Richard Michaels

I can do nothing for him.

His face is impassive, except that the sharpness of his jaw is perhaps more incisive than usual because he is clenching his teeth, exercising self-control. And when his eyes meet mine for even less than a heartbeat, is there a flicker of something—or am I just imagining that slight light because I want it to exist, because it would be a sign, however ephemeral, of what is between us? Or perhaps I am simply imagining that there is something between us? No, there is something, though I know only incompletely what it might be.

And part of that something—a very substantial part—is his cock.

His body, his almost impossibly sculpted body, is a mobile aggregation of flowing muscle and shimmering skin: the firmness of his chest with its scattering of short black hair, the conjunction of wide shoulders and rounded arms and forceful hands, all of this fleshy vista expansively spread above the thigh-length skirt, and below the skirt the revelation of his tree-trunk legs. He is solidly handsome and handsomely solid, beyond handsome, so magnetic that I am irresistibly drawn to him, and I have had to fight staring at him and expressing more than my admiration, my fascination, but also rendering entirely too obvious the connection between us.

And we had been connected two nights ago. I had knelt before him, and he had lifted the skirt, releasing his cock, his hard, hard cock, and I was on one side of the bars and he was on the other, and his risen skirt had covered the back of his prick as I covered with my yearning lips the front, and the mask shielding the head retreated, granting me full access to a masculinity as muscular as the rest of him. His hands were clenched around the bars between us, and he leaned his head against the metal, and I could tell that I was giving him pleasure.

His pleasure enhanced my own, and I found pleasure indeed in his taste and in the texture, and I wished that my ravenous tongue could reach the large low-hanging testicles, but the iron columns prevented access, and so I contented myself—no, more than contented myself—with taking his cock as fully into my mouth as I could and relishing the rough yet tender terrain and attacking each part, every part of his plentiful prick, and this was more than contenting myself; it was sating myself with the richness of his rigid manhood.

He shuddered, and I looked up, and his eyes were closed and he was biting his lower lip, trying not to create some commotion that might awaken the sleepers. He flowed into my mouth, richly and profusely, and I released myself onto the ground beneath me as I answered the quake of his body with my own.

Then, wordlessly, we separated, and he walked away, and I watched as he adjusted his skirt to cover his magnificent ass. When he had lain down with his noisily resting companions, I stood and brushed myself off and tried to erase with my foot the signs of my sexual seizure and wiped on my leg the liquid remnants from my sole, and I joined my group, and soon, lulled by the susurration of soft snoring and the warm recollection of my sensual encounter, I surrendered to sleep.

I don't know if he was there the first day or even the first week my group of captives was brought into the cell. He may have been in the forces who arrested my compatriots and me and threw us into our constricted confinement.

We had fought as well as we could, my squad and I. No one remembered how long the war had been going on. And nobody knew who was winning—although by that time, many of us, and perhaps many of them, realized that no one would really win. But no matter how many understood the futility of the combat, we, and perhaps they, comprehended that by the rules, the explicit rules, the implicit rules, neither side could retreat. Strategy had to be followed, even if the strategy was at best ambiguous and at worst injurious and most of the time impossible to discern.

So my comrades and I had been captured and incarcerated. Here we were, in an unfamiliar environment and an unfamiliar situation.

Initially, I was far too frightened to attend to my surroundings. I was jostled and jolted into a confused clump of men in the middle of our new home. We were to live here, and some of us would die here, and, according to the soldiers who had brought us, all of us would have to endure, strive to endure, pain and denial. When the soldiers told us this, the previously stony men grinned with indescribable evil.

Through the seemingly endless days that followed, we were subjected to loss, physically and emotionally, sometimes as relatively small as the withholding of meals, sometimes as great as beatings so severe that many men did not survive. And our spiritual space was more and more restrictive as we wondered what would happen to us and when and who would not make it past the next onslaught.

Our captors planted in us the seeds of fear that for some of my compatriots grew to madness, which gave our jailers great satisfaction.

In the beginning, we were stripped of our clothing. It was—it still is—a strange sensation being totally naked among many other naked men. There is so much individuality in body type and yet so universal the similarity in behaviors caused by the lack of even a minimal covering as identification, as protection. At the start, we all resolutely stared only at faces, and then no lower than chests, and soon blatantly at crotches, indulging in the masculine pastime of comparison and contrast. And then some of the glances became brazen invitations. Certain men turned away to hide what was so attractive, which presented another target for inspection and appreciation, and other men masked their own responses to invitation.

Our guards told us that anyone who succumbed to temptation would be severely punished. And no matter how clandestine the assignations, which were usually very obvious to all of us as we lay in feigned sleep and listened to the slap of flesh against flesh and the muffled cries of excitement, many were discovered by our guards, who themselves pretended slumber on the opposite side of the bars. And the transgressors were hauled away, with great ribald ceremony, not only naked but sticky and sometimes still joined, to unknown punishment. They did not return.

Self-satisfaction was frequent, and of course the satisfaction at the only permissible expression of sexual release was fleeting and not really fulfilling. The sentries laughed to hear and see men indulging in at best momentary enjoyment, and the culprits (for that is how they were made to feel) curled up in shame and pretended that they were not the ones who had surrendered to weakness. I observed these feelings not only in those around me but also in myself.

So at the beginning, I was interested only in trying to find my place in my new life, to locate some small space to call my own, some boundary within which I might discover safety, no matter how temporary, no matter how illusory. And I was not immune to the abundance of manly charms around me. My cock spent a lot of time rising and falling as if it was drawn by some strange tide, and sometimes I wanted to accede to my desires, which were often virtually uncontrollable, and yet, with an often superhuman effort, I did not give in.

And some of the other men were winsome, and some of the men were exceptionally equipped, and most tempting were the men who were both.

But I resisted—until I saw him.

He was, at first, just one of the helmeted, faceless enemy on the other side of the bars. I first noticed him in a sort of anonymous way. I looked admiringly at his remarkable legs, at their mighty size. And then he bent over to do something and revealed the splendor of his uncovered ass, which looked so solid that it could stop an arrow.

My cock sprang up and pointed at him. I quickly turned and walked to a corner of our cell where I could hide my excitement until it subsided.

He was frequently in the opposite compartment. I did not know if he was new or if he had been there all along and I had not noted him until now.

But so much more shapely were his legs than those of the other jailers that I could recognize him even behind his helmet and his armor.

One day, he removed his helmet and mopped his brow and then laid the helmet on a table, and I was nearly undone. His face was striking, with a strong jaw. When he looked my direction, before I quickly turned away, I could see—or at least I thought I could see—deep brown eyes with lustrous eyelashes, and again I had to hastily retreat to a corner of the cell until my unruly cock would behave.

You are a fool, I told myself. *You cannot possibly have seen*

*the details of his face before you retreated, and your imagination
has been overheated by your confinement, and you had better
regain control before you do something for which you will be
punished.*

For a few days, I kept myself constrained, but finally I looked
through the bars, and I found him.

And he was looking at me.

Quickly, I looked away. When I glanced back, he was talking
to another guard whom he called Marcello and who called him
Barradd. He was paying no attention to me, and I chided myself
for letting my imagination carry me into the realms of fantasy.

But the next time I let my gaze fall on him, he was again
looking at me—I was sure he was looking at me; no matter how
brief the glance, it was a glance.

Our eyes met like that two more days. Then, in the middle
of the night, something woke me, and I saw Barradd standing at
the bars, and he was wearing only his skirt. He was so beautiful
that my breath stopped for a moment.

He beckoned to me. I checked around me to be sure that
he was not gesturing to someone else—why would he choose
me, D'Meter, a lowly captive? Quite entranced by the eyes that
seemed to be drawing me to him as if he were a magnet, I stood
and walked over to him. We stared at each other for a few
seconds, and then he put his hand through the bars and guided
me to my knees and lifted his skirt, and his magnificent, munifi-
cent cock jutted toward me, and I took him in my mouth.

I was utterly enthralled by the taste of his flesh, and I lost
track of time and surroundings. Coherent thought left me, and I
was subject only to the delights of his dick.

Then he breathed heavily and shuddered and spurted into my
mouth, and I held him and his moistness for a moment, a much
too short moment, and then he withdrew and moved away and
lay down among his fellow guards, while I returned to my fellow
prisoners and fell asleep.

I was abruptly awakened by one of the guards shaking me, and when I could focus on what was happening, I saw that another guard had Barradd by the arm and was taking him to a door at one end of the bars, and this guard unlocked the door and shoved Barradd through and into the midst of us captives and said, with a nasty laugh, "You like our hostages so much, let us see how you fare among them!"

Barradd was still wearing only his skirt, and as the other guard pushed Barradd again, he pulled the skirt off, and Barradd was now, like the rest of us, completely naked.

It was obvious what had happened. Someone—another guard or a prisoner who was hoping to curry favor with his captors—had seen Barradd and me and had reported us, and now Barradd had been judged as a traitor and sentenced to be among us. Perhaps his former friends hoped that we would punish Barradd for what he was presumed to have done, might indeed have done, as a guard. Certainly Barradd would be subject to the stringent rules set for the captives.

And as I look around, I see the hatred on the faces of my fellow detainees. Barradd is one of the enemy, and now he is with us, defenseless. Here is an opportunity for revenge. Who knows what will occur later? Now is the chance to pay back some of what has happened to the prisoners.

And I can do nothing for him.

He must realize at least some of what is going to happen to him. But he refuses to show weakness; soldier that he is, he will cope with his evident fate.

But maybe I can do something for him.

So far, none of my companions knows what Barradd's offense was. What I am going to do will explain the puzzle and will simultaneously unmask me, will perhaps subject me to the same violence that Barradd would suffer.

He is not like the other soldiers. I know that. I think I know that.

I am compelled to do what I do.

I walk through the throng of bitter, vengeful men to stand before Barradd. For a moment, we look at each other. His expression is enigmatic.

"I am sorry, Barradd," I tell him, "that you and I were seen. I am sorry that you have been punished for the enjoyment we took in each other. But I am not sorry that no more do bars separate us. Being so close to you allows me to do this."

Does Barradd desire this? Is there indeed something between us? Am I delusional? Whatever the reality may be, in my lunacy, I kneel and take his cock in my mouth.

And part of me protests. Why am I doing this? Have I been stricken with a streak of insanity? Am I so overcome with lust that I lose all caution? Do I want this man so much that I am willing to risk—what? What happens as a result of this may be more dire than any revenge my compatriots might have leveled against him before. And by doing this, I probably, almost certainly, absolutely certainly, will subject myself to severe measures I could avoid if I just constrained myself.

His cock is as before plenteous in taste and generous in girth and length, and I could quite happily suck on it for days. And this time, I can reach his testicles, large, heavy sacs that smell of sweat and sexual potency, and I bury my nose in them and inhale deeply, and my own cock becomes achingly hard.

After a while, I let go of him and look up at him and smile. He seems somewhat puzzled.

I turn around so that I am facing away from him and bend over, presenting my rear end to him and presuming that he will know what to do with it.

For a moment, nothing happens, and I begin to think that I have misestimated the situation.

Then there is movement behind me, and he drops his hands on my back, and I feel the head of his cock at my asshole. He inserts himself.

My ass is not unexplored territory, but suddenly it feels almost virginal. Maybe I have not correctly judged my ability to take him, because his intrusion is painful, and I almost want to tell him, "This was a bad idea," but as he slowly slides in and out of me, the pain decreases and pleasure takes its place.

His cock is certainly the largest and thickest that has gained admission to my ass. He might presume that, because his motions are slow and steady, as if he is allowing me to get used to his size. I get used to it. And I like it. Very much.

I stare at the men who stare at Barradd and me, and in the moment of coherent thought that is given to me, I wonder again why I am doing this. Am I rebelling against this crowd who might become a mob, rebelling against not only them but my family and the inhabitants of my village who could not hide their dismay at me and my actions? Is this a challenge to whatever is in charge of my fate, since I no longer seem to be in control? Is this a hunger that has overtaken me?

And what is going through Barradd's mind? Has he considered what penalty he might incur from the other guards as he consorts with the enemy? Is he just as driven as I by instincts and desires beyond repression? I like to think that I have a fetching ass, but is it so fetching that it has impelled him to cast aside discretion just to possess me?

I arch my back to give him encouragement, and his tempo picks up, and soon he is driving all the way into me and then withdrawing almost completely, and he is warming me and expanding me. As he thrusts forward, I thrust backward, meeting his hips with a jolt. His stroke increases in speed, and now we are well beyond the tentative exploration; now he is truly fucking me.

I feel the scrape of his crotch hair against my ass, and it seems that the intensity and the friction is burning its way from my buttocks down through his cock and igniting my insides, not just the path that his prick is invading and capturing and making every part of my body entirely and utterly his as he drives into me.

I look up. Some of the men watching us are smiling, and some are openmouthed, and some are visibly excited, and some are stroking themselves.

Barradd goes faster and faster, and his hands press down against my back, and then he bends over me and propels himself into me, striking my ass with so much force that I can maintain my balance no longer, and I fall and then I lie beneath him as he batters and pummels me, and his breath is hot on my neck, and I hear both of us puffing and panting, echoed by the sighs and moans of the men surrounding us.

Can he fuck me faster? He does.

Can he fuck me harder? He does.

And I revel in the pounding, hammering assault, and I cry out to him, "Faster! Harder!"

And he goes faster and harder until I nearly become one with the earth beneath me.

Then he shouts, and he floods into me, and I match his yell and pour into the ground below. He collapses on top of me, and we remain that way, not wanting to move, not able to move.

We shall have to move, because two of the guards, two of his former fellows, roughly lift us to our feet. They are laughing as they inspect our sticky steamy bodies, and they shake their heads.

"Let's go," one of them says. "You know what happens now."

No, I do not. But I am going to find out.

Perhaps Barradd knows what happens now, what will happen when we leave the cage and go through the door.

We go through the door.

To our fate.

THE ORKNEY LANDING

Brent Archer

Harald Sigurdsen stood overlooking the craggy Orkney coast-
line. Far below him, the longboat rested beside the rocks and
bobbed in the calm surf. The storm earlier in the morning had
given way to bright sunshine, and the sea had calmed consider-
ably, making it possible for the small raiding party to land.

Thorjus Halvorsen climbed over the last of the stones from
the rough path up the side of the cliff. "It is a grand day to fight
these barbarian Picts."

Harald clasped the shoulder of the rugged Viking beside him.
"We shall spill their blood today, my friend."

"Look there."

Harald's gaze followed the direction Thorjus pointed in as
the other ten warriors joined them. Across the peat- and heather-
covered moorland, a column of smoke rose from the center of a
house surrounded by farmland. He addressed his soldiers. "Our
first conquest. Draw your weapons."

The Norsemen raised their swords and hammers with a cheer.

Harald returned his attention to the farm. "Forward!"

Running toward the settlement, Harald deeply inhaled the Orkney air. *Fresh and clean. I'll enjoy conquering this land.*

Several Picts ran over the hill behind the farm toward them. The door to the house opened, and a tall man with flaming-red hair clutched a thick club as he charged. Behind him, a middle-aged woman and three children fled from the house over the hill.

Harald counted his opponents. *Twenty, and most of them look to be unskilled savages. An easy battle.* He ran his sword through the first of the defenders to reach him. His comrades made short work of the Picts with two remaining men fleeing from the battlefield.

Thorjus pointed at them. "Pursue the rogues. No survivors. Then return and make camp for the night."

The ten warriors hurried off to slay the remaining Picts.

Harald settled his gaze on the farm. "Ready?"

Thorjus gripped his sword with a grin.

The two Vikings stormed into the round house. Harald spied a cooking pot over a fire in the center of the room, a bed against the wall to the left and a table to the right with five chairs. A large tapestry hung from two wooden pillars.

He turned to Thorjus. "Burn it. The owner's dead anyway."

A gasp echoed around the room as the tapestry ruffled.

Harald strode to the two heavy timbers and tore the colorful cloth away from the wall. Behind it, a shivering man of about twenty years cowered in the curve of the wall. His tattered clothes indicated a servant of some sort. *The lad is handsome. A noble nose and chin under his red curls.*

Thorjus stepped forward. "What have we here?"

"A mouse." Harald held his sword to the man's throat. "Squeak, mouse. Tell us your name."

The Pict's eyes bulged, fear dancing across his face. "E...E... Eivind."

Thorjus's eyes widened. "He understands us."

"My master taught me the Norse language."

Harald removed the metal from the young man's neck. "How?"

"He learned from a Viking merchant their raiding party took captive and taught it to me to care for the slave."

Thorjus crossed his arms and towered over the terrified man. "Where is this Norse trader?"

"Dead. A month ago."

Harald turned to his comrade. "What do you think?"

The other Viking nodded. "Kill him."

Harald returned his stare to the Pict on the floor. His frame was slender but strong. A handsome youth with captivating green eyes. Warmth rushed through him. *What is it about this man that makes me hesitate?* "No. Bind him. We may take him with us for a slave."

Thorjus shook his head. "You know we must travel light to keep the element of surprise with the local savages. We have no provisions to keep a captive."

"I'll decide in the morning."

Thorjus bustled Eivind outside the small house. He returned a few moments later. "I left him beside the house with a blanket over him. Will you keep him?"

"Perhaps. If he can be broken to serve us and not run away, he'd be useful for watching our supplies and making our meals."

Thorjus slid the leather armor from his chest. "Now we can relax for the night."

Harald nodded. "This is a good place to sleep, and the men will be well rested for the next battle. We'll burn it before we leave." His gaze ran the length of his mate's muscular chest, following the trail of hair from his belly button to his bulging crotch. Heat brought his cock to hardness. "So, my warrior, will you give yourself to me tonight?"

Thorjus stiffened. "You wish me to take the submissive role?"

Harald grabbed the stiffness poking from the trousers of his companion. "The thought excites you."

"Your touch excites me." Thorjus leaned forward, bringing his hand to Harald's hair and pulling his head closer. "Take me if you can." He mashed their lips together, his tongue prodding for entry to duel with Harald's.

His grip on Thorjus's cock slackened as he closed his eyes, surrendering to the lip-lock. Their trimmed beards brushed together and their kiss increased in passion. *Very well. I'll take you, warrior.* Harald regained some of his control as he slowly opened Thorjus's trousers and tugged them down. He slid his palm over the foreskin, eliciting a moan from Thorjus as he continued to press his tongue against Harald's lips.

Thorjus dropped his hands to his sides as Harald stroked him. "You're making my knees shake."

Harald grinned. "I'll make your whole body tremble before I'm finished with you." He placed his hands on Thorjus's shoulders and shoved him onto the small bed. Locking his gaze with his comrade's blue eyes, he stripped out of his armor and trousers and threw them onto the floor. He unwrapped his leggings and kicked off his shoes, then descended onto the bed, pinning Thorjus to the fur skins covering the straw-stuffed mattress.

Thorjus struggled, but then wrapped his legs around Harald's waist. "Make your conquest complete."

Harald's cock throbbed as he held Thorjus's hands over his head. "You're mine, Viking." He spit into one hand and slicked the blond warrior's pucker, peeling back the skin covering the already slippery head of Thorjus's dick. Harald pressed forward.

The muscular man arched his back and Harald moved inside him. "*Aaahh...*"

Harald fought the urge to shoot as he held still, fully lodged in his lover's ass. "Nod when you're ready."

Thorjus squeezed his hairy legs around Harald's waist and pressed his heels into the other man's ass. He nodded as he tightened his sphincter.

Pleasure crashed through Harald as his balls tingled. *It won't be long tonight.* He pulled his shaft back until only the head remained inside, then slammed forward.

Harald smirked as Thorjus gripped his hand and spread his legs wider.

"More."

The fire of lust blazed inside Harald, and he set a hard, pounding rhythm. He released Thorjus's hands and slid his own under his lover's shoulders. Pummeling the blond man's ass, he leaned forward to kiss the moaning Thorjus and stroke his stiffness.

The tingling in his balls intensified, and Harald drove harder. His fingers flew over the head of Thorjus's cock. The man beneath him shook and roared as blast after blast of thick come sprayed between them, coating Thorjus's blond chest hair in white ropes.

As the orgasm raged through Thorjus, his ass muscles tightened and milked Harald over the edge. He slammed in one last time, yelled and threw his head back as he released inside his warrior lover.

Thorjus wrapped his arms around Harald's back and pulled him down and into a gentle kiss. "An excellent conquest."

Slipping from Thorjus's hole, Harald rose and found a jug of water. He grabbed a rag from the floor next to the table and dunked it into the cold liquid, then brought it back to rub the sticky mess from their chests.

He threw the cloth onto the floor, and then curled up next to Thorjus. "Get some sleep. Tomorrow to battle."

Thorjus rested his head on Harald's chest and closed his eyes.

As Harald settled on the bed, his thoughts drifted to the Pict outside as he surrendered to his drowsiness. *Eivind. A handsome name for a handsome lad. Will I let him live?*

Harald awoke to the sound of rain pelting against the roof of the house. Thorjus lightly snored next to him. He traced the patterns of straw-colored hair swirling over the muscular chest of the sleeping warrior. Pressure built in his bladder, and he pushed himself up.

Standing, he strode out the door and around the side of the house. Cold rain beat against his skin as he let loose a stream. *Time to wake Thorjus so we can get moving. These Picts may have been alerted to our presence if that woman and her children survived the night.* He finished and turned his attention farther along the side of the house.

The huddled form of the sleeping servant shivered under the soaked blanket in the cold rain. Harald stalked to him and kicked the side of his hip. "Wake up." He reached down, ripped the cords securing his legs and pulled the young man's hair as he struggled to stand.

He glanced across the ramshackle fence in front of the dwelling. Five tents with posts carved with runes and dragon heads stood beyond the entrance. The sentry waved to him. *I'll wake the rest of the men after some breakfast.*

Harald marched the slave into the house and shoved him to the floor. He grabbed a knife from the table and cut the bindings from around his captive's hands. "Make food for us. If you try to run, I'll chase you down, run my sword through your spine and leave you to die, starving and unable to move."

Eivind's eyes bulged as he gasped and nodded. "Yes, Lord Viking."

Harald kept an eye on the Pict as he returned to the bed and, kneeling, placed a hand on Thorjus's shoulder. "Wake up. We need to prepare."

His comrade sat up, immediately awake. "Good morning." He glanced toward the fumbling servant. "You released him?"

"He's preparing our breakfast."

Thorjus turned back to Eivind. "He has a fine form."

Harald's gaze raked over the young man. *I know what we must do. My lust can't endanger our raid.* He addressed Thorjus.

"True, but we can't afford to bring him. We'll leave his corpse in the house when we burn it."

Eivind dropped a pottery bowl. Harald turned to him as he brought his hand to the sword lying on the floor.

"My apologies, Lord Viking. See, there is bread on the table, and I've started a fire to warm the stew." Eivind pointed to the metal pot over a small fire in the middle of the room.

Harald gripped his sword and strode quickly across the room to grab the Pict by the hair, pushing him to the floor. "We leave no survivors." Regret streamed through him as he glared into the green eyes of the kneeling man.

"I heard your coupling last night. Please, Lord Viking, I have a desire to feel a man move inside me, and hope you will allow me to live long enough to give myself to you as your slave."

Harald froze, eyeing the Pict suspiciously as a surge of desire gripped him. "Is this some trick or a plea for your life?"

The redheaded man shook his head. "No. Kill me afterward if you wish. I don't fear death, but only desire to go to the next world having known the pleasures of another man."

Harald held his sword at the servant's neck and turned to Thorjus.

His lover returned his glance and shrugged. "What harm could it do? He's giving himself willingly to us."

Harald nodded, lowering his sword. "Very well. We'll take you with us. Remember my threat if you try to escape. If, at the end of the day we aren't dead, we'll show you how men pleasure each other." He turned to Thorjus. "Get dressed. We'll torch the house after we eat."

Harald stomped across the heather and returned to the stake where Thorjus had bound Eivind earlier that afternoon. Their captive rested on the ground, arms wrapped around the metal pole. *It doesn't look like he even tried to escape.* Eivind met his gaze as he approached.

"You're still here."

"Yes, Lord Viking."

"You understand the danger you're in?"

He nodded. "I know you'll kill me when you're done with me."

Harald towered over the smaller man. *What is it about this man that's different from all the others we've killed yesterday and today?* He stooped down and ran his hand through the man's red hair and down his stubble-covered jaw. "Do you still wish to feel a man inside you?"

"Yes. A real warrior like you."

Thorjus trotted up to them, standing beside Harald. "The men have set up camp. We're secure for the night."

Harald cut Eivind's bindings from around his wrists. "Good. Our Pict still wants a taste of Viking cock."

Thorjus rubbed his hands together. "The tent is ready."

Harald pulled Eivind to his feet. "Follow Thorjus."

Thorjus led the way with Eivind between them. The vision of the young Pict's lean body filled Harald with warmth. His cock hardened in his trousers. *Such a handsome man. His round ass was made for fucking.*

Eivind glanced behind him. He lowered his eyes, and then returned his gaze forward.

A few minutes later, they arrived at the camp. Thorjus pushed back the fabric of the entrance. He entered, followed by Eivind.

Harald turned to observe the evening sky. The sun set behind a low row of clouds covering the horizon, coloring it a light pink. A stiff breeze blew across the moorland, whipping his hair across his face. *A beautiful night.* He stepped into the tent and pulled the flap shut.

Eivind stripped and lay naked on a rug. Thorjus pulled his cock from his trousers and lodged it into his throat. The young man struggled to take more.

Thorjus grinned. "He's eager. His prior master must have

starved him of sex." He moaned as Eivind sucked him.

Heat flooded Harald's body, and his dick pulsed. Quickly stripping out of his armor and clothes, he approached the bed and presented his cock to the handsome servant. *Just a light dusting of red hair on his chest.* Eivind's long cock bobbed as he continued to pleasure Thorjus.

The blond Viking stepped back, his cock leaving Eivind's mouth with a popping sound. "Feed him while I undress."

Harald ran his hand along Eivind's stubbled cheek. "Pleasure me."

Eivind gently caressed Harald's balls as he licked the shaft. Prickles of sensation flew across Harald's skin, and he shook with a burst of pleasure. Eivind's tongue teased the opening of his foreskin, then dove in and slid around the head as he pulled the cock into his mouth.

Harald groaned. *So good.*

Thorjus joined him and slipped his arm across his shoulder. "Do you wish to take his virginity, or shall I?"

Another hard suck and a light tug at his balls made Harald step back as his shaft hardened. "I want it." He knelt between the young man's legs and lifted them, spitting onto Eivind's pucker and pressing his cock against it. "Are you ready?"

Fear danced in Eivind's eyes, but he nodded.

"I'll be gentle with you, as this is your first time." He slowly thrust forward.

Eivind gasped, his eyes wide as the head of Harald's cock breached his hole.

Harald paused. "Breathe deep." He pressed forward again, filling the servant with the entire length of his shaft.

Eivind clutched at the blanket. Small whimpers accompanied each deep breath.

Harald fought the urge to fuck the Pict hard. He ran his hand across Eivind's chest and pinched the erect nipples, making him clutch Harald's cock with his ass muscles while he panted.

Eivind grasped Harald's arm. "The pain is ebbing."

"It will pass completely in a few moments." He pulled back and eased forward, establishing a slow rhythm. Soon, Eivind moaned and clamped his hands on Harald's legs.

"More."

Thorjus kneeled on the tent floor over Eivind's head. "Suck me while my man fucks you."

Harald leaned forward and sucked one of Thorjus's nipples as he plowed the moaning man beneath him. His cock hardened watching the young man spit roasted between them and drilled deep as his balls tingled.

"I'm close."

Thorjus stood, pulling his hardness from Eivind's mouth. "Slowly. I don't want this to end just yet."

Harald fought back the urge to shoot, pausing in his fucking. He widened his eyes as Thorjus slipped behind him and pressed his cock against Harald's ass.

"What are you doing?"

"What does it feel like?" He thrust into Harald, wrapping his arm around Harald's chest.

A slight stinging accompanied his swift entry, but quickly gave way to pleasure as Thorjus jammed his cock against the sensitive spot inside him. Eivind gripped Harald's cock harder with his ass and squealed as Thorjus pressed into Harald.

"Oh fuck."

Thorjus increased his speed, driving Harald deep into the redhaired man beneath him.

Eivind's head whipped back and he howled as his cock fired several white streams across his lean chest.

The pulsing of Eivind's ass and the pounding of Thorjus's cock drove Harald over the edge and his orgasm racked his body. He came inside the shuddering man as Thorjus roared his release behind him and tightened his grip across Harald's chest.

Harald's cock softened and he pulled out of Eivind before rolling to the side and dislodging Thorjus from his ass. He sucked in large breaths of air as his racing heart slowed to normal.

Thorjus retrieved a cloth and wetted it with water from a bowl that sat on a small barrel. He wiped off his cock, then cleaned Harald and wiped the mess from Eivind's body. Tossing the rag on the floor, he returned to the two men.

Harald raised an eyebrow as he stared at Eivind. "Well?"

Eivind smiled. "I can die happy now."

Harald rested his arm across the lean man. He grinned. "You're not going to die by our hands."

Thorjus joined them, pressing his body against Eivind's back. "You did well. We'll protect you from harm."

Eivind nestled his head onto Harald's hairy pec. "Thank you."

Harald stroked Eivind's hair and pressed his lips to Thorjus's. "Good night. To battle in the morning."

The next day, after a breakfast of rations, Harald directed Eivind in the efficient packing of the tent and its contents as Thorjus looked on.

"Be quick. It's time to move forward." Harald stepped from the tent into the crisp morning air.

Eivind finished the packing and carried a large bag of supplies as the other Vikings disassembled the camp. "Ready, Lord Viking."

Two of the closest warriors glanced at Eivind and then to Harald with a smirk.

"You men have something to say?"

Both of their faces reddened. "No, Harald. We're only admiring your new slave."

Harald bristled for a moment, and Thorjus placed a hand on his shoulder. He relaxed and smiled. "He's a quick learner."

He watched Eivind lift the bag of supplies, his slender muscles straining. *Why did that bother me? He's a slave. A willing slave, but a slave nonetheless.*

Shaking off his confusion, he focused on the march at hand. The raiding party covered several leagues over the hilly countryside, burning farmhouses as they went. At each dwelling, Harald paused to look inside.

After they plundered their fourteenth farm, he shook his head as he lit a torch. *Each house deserted. This doesn't bode well for the stealth of our assault.*

Before he could light the thatched roof, a cheer arose from a far-off hill. He dropped the torch and turned to his company. The men crowded behind him, facing the oncoming attack.

Gray clouds descended as Harald counted the naked Pict men painted blue, wielding swords and clubs and surging across the moor. *Twenty-seven. These look more like warriors. The farm woman or the children survived and sounded the alarm.* He turned to his men. "Torvald, Andreas and Halvor, take the savages on the right. Erik, Tallak and Sigurd, take the left. The rest of you with me and Thorjus down the center."

Turning, he brought his attention to Eivind. "Hide amongst the supplies. If the battle goes ill, run. If you're needed, you will hear two blasts of my horn."

"Yes, my lord." Eivind scurried to the pile of wood for the tents and ducked out of sight.

Harald raised his sword as the rain fell and a peel of thunder rolled over the moor. "Forward, and take no prisoners!"

He roared as they ran toward the approaching savages. Excitement surged through his veins, and he slashed his sword at the lead Pict, slicing the life from him. Another swung a club at him, but he missed. He dispatched the fiery-haired man with a single stroke.

Harald looked on with satisfaction as more of the Picts fell to the Vikings' swords. He stabbed another man in the shoulder, and the savage fell. Turning toward another, he thrust the blade through the attacker.

"Harald, look out!"

Thorjus's warning came too late. Pain ripped through his leg as a club smashed his ankle. He gripped his sword and stabbed it through the Pict who'd previously swung at him, and then he fell, clutching his legging in agony.

The five Vikings around him formed a defensive shield with their bodies and dispatched most of the remaining attackers. Through the pain, Harald spied five Picts running.

"I'm all right. Finish those bastards."

Thorjus knelt beside him as the others pursued their quarry. "We need to get you to safety so the wound can be cleansed." He took the horn hanging from his waist and blew two shrill notes.

A few moments later, Eivind ran to them. "Lord Viking, you are injured."

Thorjus nodded. "Help me lift him. We'll take him into the farmhouse."

Harald grunted when they lifted him as pain surged up his leg. He gripped Thorjus's shoulder as his Viking lover slung his arm across Harald's back. "It's not far."

Eivind ran ahead and opened the door to the farmhouse. "Bring him inside. There's a bed."

Harald glanced around the room. *Sufficient.* He howled as Thorjus eased him onto the bed.

"Rest, my love. Eivind, fetch something to help him."

Eivind rifled through the contents of the house and came to Thorjus with cuttings from two plants. "This will cleanse the wound and ease some of the pain." The servant uncovered the wound and added herbs. "The bleeding has stopped, Lord Viking."

Harald grumbled as he lay on the bed. He glanced at his leggings stained with blood and his wounded ankle. *You fool. Should've known that savage wasn't dead.*

Thorjus paced the room. "We need you to lead us, Harald. The raid can't continue without you."

He assessed the injury. *The Pict was too good. I'll not fight again until this is healed.* "Eivind, fetch a small smooth piece of wood. Whittle it smooth and pierce it. Leave space for two runes."

Eivind pulled a small knife from the table and hurried outside.

Harald lifted his head and bored his gaze into his comrade's blue eyes. "You must lead. The king made our objectives clear. The men will follow you."

"But what of *you*?"

"Eivind will attend me. This house is sufficient for our needs, and I can recover."

The blond Viking crossed his arms. "Can you trust him?" He nodded toward Eivind.

The Pict stiffened as he strode through the doorway. "I could have killed both of you in your sleep several times, and instead of fleeing, I came when you called." He handed the smooth piece of wood to Harald and gave him the knife. "I'll care for him."

Harald carved a perfect X into the wood on one side of the hole, and a Y with a line running through the middle of it on the other. He pressed the knife into his blood-soaked leggings and scraped it over the lines of the runes, turning them red.

Thorjus raised an eyebrow. "*Gebo* and *Algiz*."

"Partnership and Protection." He tied the runes to the Viking's leather armor. "Go, while you have the light."

"Serve your master well, Eivind. He's very important to me." Thorjus knelt beside Harald. "Get well so you can return to fight with us."

Harald ran his fingers along the blond hairs of Thorjus's beard, smiling as he gazed into the warrior's blue eyes. "I can't recover quick enough from this wound to be of any use to our raiders. I'd just slow your progress."

Thorjus hardened his gaze. "I'll return for you when we've tamed this land and its savages. The longboats should be here soon with more warriors. We light the signal fires tonight." He stood and strode to the door. He pressed his fist to the talisman on his chest. "My love."

Pain radiated from Harald's heart as he watched Thorjus leave the house.

"Don't worry, Lord Viking, he'll return."

"I've no doubt of it." Harald shifted his gaze to Eivind. "And you must refer to me as Harald." He held his arm out, and the Pict sat next to the bed.

"Yes, Lord Harald."

Harald sat at the table eating a bowl of Eivind's stew and musing over the nearly two years they'd lived together. *He is a good companion.* He sipped at the warm broth. *And his cooking rivals any I've had before.* He cast his gaze at Eivind as the young man stared out of a window.

"Lord Thorjus is approaching the house."

Harald's heart leapt. *Perhaps he's through with battle at last. Two years is enough time apart.* He stood from his chair and limped to the door, his ankle permanently damaged from the Pict's blow.

Eivind opened the door and bowed.

"Good lad, Eivind." Thorjus clasped the young man's shoulder, then turned to face Harald. "Hello, my love."

Harald stood tall. "How goes the conquest?"

"Well." Thorjus approached him as Eivind closed the door. "We have taken most of the surrounding lands, and waves of Norse settlers established a town not far from here." He ran a hand along Harald's face, causing a shiver to run down Harald's spine.

"I've missed you."

"And I you. I've been on the front lines of our assault, but have returned as I promised." Thorjus cocked his head to the side and furrowed his brow. "You're clean shaven."

Heat rushed to Harald's face. "I shave for Eivind. He prefers my face without the beard."

Thorjus chuckled. "Indeed. Who's the master and who's the slave?"

A flare of anger shook Harald, and he narrowed his eyes. "I don't see a slave here. Only a loyal servant and companion."

Thorjus's eyes widened. "Then much has changed in two years."

Harald turned and hobbled to his chair.

"Please, Lord Thorjus, we're happy here." Eivind approached their guest. "Let me rekindle your memory of the first night we were all together."

Harald suppressed a smile as Eivind unlaced Thorjus's armor. Thorjus raised an eyebrow, but made no attempt to move away from the Pict. After carefully placing the leather on the table, he pulled each of the warrior's leather shoes off and unwound his leg wrapping as Thorjus balanced with his large hand resting on the servant's shoulder.

Harald's cock hardened. *He's even more muscular than I remember.*

Eivind continued to undress the Viking until he stood before them completely naked. Dropping to his knees, the redheaded Pict sucked the quickly rising cock before him into his mouth. Thorjus moaned and rested his hand on the back of the young man's head.

"I'd forgotten how good this feels."

Harald stroked his cock through his trousers as he watched Eivind bob on Thorjus. "Have you not enjoyed the spoils of conquest and taken someone?"

Thorjus stroked Eivind's hair as he locked his gaze with Harald. "No one since you remained here." He pulled on Eivind's hair. "Enough. I don't want to release too soon."

Eivind stood and returned to Harald's side. "Allow me." He lifted Harald's tunic over his head and untied the belt around the baggy trousers. As the fabric fell, his cock slapped against his abdomen.

Thorjus whistled. "Impressive as ever."

Eivind sank to his knees and engulfed the head into his mouth, sending ripples of pleasure through Harald's shaft. He thrust forward with a loud groan to embed his dick into Eivind's throat.

Thorjus stepped forward to stand next to Harald, his hardness pressing against Eivind's face as he continued to suck.

I've had the comfort and pleasure of Eivind while my Thorjus denied himself for me. Harald wrapped an arm around the Viking's shoulder, guilt racing through him. "You've truly been with no one since we parted?"

"I haven't wanted anyone else, though I'm glad Eivind was here to attend to your needs." Thorjus leaned toward Harald and placed a rough kiss on his lips.

Harald squirmed between the passionate force of the lip-lock and the tickling of Thorjus's trimmed beard. He returned the fervor of the kiss, squeezing the man next to him and thrusting into Eivind's mouth.

Eivind released Harald's cock and stood, placing light kisses on Harald's neck.

Harald held onto Thorjus as his knees weakened from the pleasure the two men gave him. "A moment to catch my breath."

Thorjus took his arm. "Perhaps we should move to the bed so you may rest while we resume our passion."

Harald intertwined his fingers with Eivind's as the younger man led the way to the bed. Once there, Eivind stripped and lay on top of the blankets.

Thorjus nodded. "You're a handsome man. It's good we didn't kill you when we found you behind that tapestry." He lay on the bed next to Eivind, and they both stared at Harald.

Harald admired the differences in their bodies. Eivind's slender yet sturdy frame and lightly haired chest contrasted with the blond swirls covering the stocky body of the rugged

Norseman. Thorjus's thick erection pressed against a blond trail leading from his belly button to his large balls. The young Pict's cock, though not nearly as large in girth, was longer, and it rose from a tuft of red hair around its base.

His mouth watered as he lowered himself onto the bed and kissed his way along Thorjus's hairy leg. He gazed into the Norseman's blue eyes as he licked up the man's shaft and engulfed the head with his mouth.

Thorjus laid his head back with his mouth open as Eivind kissed his neck. Harald concentrated on sucking Thorjus's cock and getting it as wet as he could. The muscular legs beneath him straightened and squeezed him between them.

Eivind licked along Thorjus's jaw and planted a lingering kiss onto his lips. As he groaned, Thorjus shook. His balls rose and his shaft hardened.

Not yet. Harald pulled his mouth away from the throbbing cock and spit into his hand. He rubbed the tips of his fingers around and into his ass, then he straddled Thorjus's hips. Lining up the cock beneath him to his hole, Harald pressed down as the head of Thorjus's cock impaled him. A jolt of pain shot through Harald as Thorjus thrust upward.

"You're tight."

Harald closed his eyes for a moment and took a deep breath, the sting lessening. "No one but you has been inside me."

Eivind moved from Thorjus's lips to Harald's dick. "It's true, Lord Thorjus." He slid the shaft into his mouth as Harald rode his lover's erection.

The surge of pleasure through Harald intensified as his balls tingled. "I'm close."

Eivind released Harald's cock. "Inside me." He turned and pressed his ass against Harald's hardness.

Harald's dick pulsed as he slid into Eivind, and soon he rode the wave of his orgasm, hugging the redheaded man against his chest as he fired off inside him.

Thorjus pulled out of Harald and gently pulled Eivind from his arms. He spun the Pict around and bent him forward. Harald held him as Thorjus pressed inside his ass.

"Yes, Lord Thorjus. I want it. Give it to me."

Thorjus pounded him, then rammed in hard and threw his head back with a groan as his hand clasped Eivind's shoulder. "Here it is." Each small thrust accompanied a grunt as Thorjus came inside Eivind.

Harald stroked the young man's hair and kissed his forehead.

Eivind sighed. "I truly belong to both of you."

Harald wrapped his arms around both of them, and his two lovers rested their heads on his chest. "Let's get some sleep."

Harald woke to an insistent nudging at his ass. His arm rested over the still sleeping Eivind while Thorjus pressed against his back. Harald pulled at his asscheeks to allow Thorjus's cock easy access to his hole.

Thorjus chuckled. "Good morning." He spit into his hand and rubbed it onto the head of his dick. "I want to have you. May I?"

"Take me."

A slight sting accompanied intense pleasure as Thorjus gently eased into Harald's ass. He clutched Eivind tighter as he grew accustomed to Thorjus's hardness sliding inside him.

Eivind sighed, but didn't wake.

Thorjus continued to fuck Harald with a gentle rhythm. Not too slow or fast, but enough to make Harald's erection throb with each thrust. After a few moments, Thorjus's rhythm faltered, and he buried his cock deep inside Harald as he bit his shoulder and groaned. He shook as his dick throbbed.

Shuddering as his softened cock slipped from Harald's hole, Thorjus held him for a few moments as his breath slowed to normal. "Two years was too long to wait."

Harald turned his head toward his lover. "You don't have to leave right away, do you?"

Thorjus pushed himself up onto his elbow, his head resting on his hand. "No. The invasion's complete. I'm ready to settle down."

"What of your career as a fighter?"

Thorjus chuckled. "I've had two years to think about it. There's honor in tending the land. This soil is rich, and I want to be with you if you want me."

Happiness flooded Harald. "Of course I want you. Stay with us."

Thorjus carefully slipped from the bed and retrieved something from his armor. He pressed it into Harald's hand as he returned to the bed.

Harald turned the wooden disc in his hand. "The runes."

"I wouldn't have made it through without this talisman."

Harald pressed his back against Thorjus's body as he hugged Eivind close. Thorjus wrapped his arm around him and kissed his neck.

My warrior is home.

RISE UP

B. Snow

Dedicated to those who died during the Warsaw Ghetto Uprising, April–June, 1943, and to those who lived through it.

Warsaw
April 22, 1943

"Grenades. Where do you want them?" Stan hefted the crate, praying he wouldn't drop it.

"Second doorway on the left." The man he'd been told to ask walked past him without even a look.

"That's gratitude," Stan muttered.

"Hey, fuck you!"

Stan looked over his shoulder. His heartbeat sped up as the man marched back toward him, the thick, dark brows drawn low, mouth set in a snarl. "All I said was—"

"You think you're doing us some kind of favor, bringing weapons into the ghetto?" The man walked right up to Stan, leaning in so they were face-to-face, so close that the smell of barley puffed in warm bursts across Stan's chin with every angry word. "*We're* the ones doing *you* a favor! As long as the Nazis are focused on this place, you and your resistance buddies can do whatever you like."

Stan set the crate down and let out a breath. "Yeah, us Poles are having a great time. It's like one big party outside these walls. In fact, I won these grenades at the Gestapo Field Day. No one can beat me at the wheelbarrow race." He glared at the man, who went still, staring at Stan with an unreadable expression for so long that Stan thought maybe he'd died standing upright.

"Are we finished here?" the man finally said.

"Yeah."

"All right." He turned and walked away.

Stan watched him for a few seconds, then let out a disgusted sound and picked up the crate again. As he turned into the second doorway, he heard a "Thank you," from the far end of the alley. Or maybe it was just the sound of a door closing.

April 27, 1943

Stan stood in the same alley with another crate. "Bottles. You can use them for—"

"We know how to make Molotov cocktails," the man said, taking the crate from Stan and walking away.

Stan fell into step beside him. "What's your name?"

"Why do you want to know? Are you a German spy?"

"Yes," Stan said, sarcasm clinging to the word. "I'm a German spy who brings you weapons because I like to keep things *interesting*."

And there, the expression dropped right off the man's face again. Then he scowled. "You *look* German. A perfect example of the Aryan superman."

Stan ran a hand over his short blond hair. "It's how I get through the city. I put on a German uniform. None of them even look twice at me in the street."

"Shit! That's dangerous!"

Finally, something other than scorn or boredom. "It's *all* dangerous," Stan countered. "You're a bunch of Jews standing up to the army of the Third Reich in the middle of a country full of people who would just as soon hand you over."

"But *you* wouldn't."

"Like you said, you're distracting the Nazis for us."

"Is that the only reason you're helping us?" The man handed the crate off to a group of women and continued walking, Stan at his side.

Stan shrugged. "I've always rooted for the underdog." He held out his hand. "Stanislav. My friends call me Stan. I've been with the Polish Resistance for almost a year."

The man scowled again, but he took Stan's hand and shook it. "Yakov. Thanks for the bottles, *Stanislav*."

Well, it was a kind of progress.

May 2, 1943

"Here." Stan held out a cloth-wrapped packet. "Bread and cheese. Eat it."

Yakov took it and tossed it on the bed. "I'll have it later."

"Have it now."

"I'm not hungry."

"You damn well are, and you're going to eat it while I watch, not give it away to someone else."

Yakov sneered, the hair on his unshaven upper lip bunching up into a dark line. "I don't have to do a damn thing, you arrogant—"

"Tomasz took some to the kids, so you don't have to give yours away to them. I know you do that."

"You don't know anything."

"Then it's a damn good guess." Stan reached out and grabbed Yakov by the shirt collar. "Right there," he said, pressing his hand against Yakov's ribs. "No meat on those bones."

Yakov shoved him away. "It's none of your damned business."

"How do you expect to protect these people if you're dead from hunger?"

After a long silence, Yakov swore and picked up the package. "Fine," he said, unwrapping it. "But you'll share it with me."

"I've already eaten."

"But you could eat more." Yakov stretched his hand out, slipped it inside Stan's coat, pressed against Stan's ribs. "Not much meat on those bones, either."

Stan shivered, but kept his eyes locked on Yakov's.

Yakov removed his hand, broke off a piece of bread and handed it to Stan.

Stan took it. It smelled a bit like the gun oil smudged on the tips of Yakov's long, slim fingers, but he ate it anyway. He watched Yakov bite, chew, swallow. After a minute or so, a boy of about thirteen stepped into the room. "Yakov, I—" He started, gasping, his eyes going wide when he saw Stan. He stumbled back a step, bumping into an older woman who had been following close behind.

"Oh! You've got company," the woman said, steadying the boy.

A girl stepped out from behind her. "Hi, Yaki. Who's your friend?"

"None of your business, Ruthie. Channah." Yakov nodded at the woman. "What do you need?"

"Sollie forgot his tallis." She nudged the boy forward. He eyed Stan nervously, then snatched a cloth pouch off a shelf.

"Wait." Yakov broke off some of the bread and cheese, handing it to the boy. "Now get lost."

The boy shot out of the room, clutching the food.

"You, too," he said to Channah, holding out more bread and cheese as he spoke.

"Thank you," she said, passing it to Ruthie. When Yakov

broke off another piece of bread, she waved it away. "I just ate. We'll leave you men alone to discuss strategy." She left, pulling the door closed behind her.

"What's a tallis?" Stan asked.

"Prayer shawl. He's no good with a gun, so I told him to pray for us."

"I didn't figure you for a religious man."

"I'm not. And it gives him something to do. Can't have some useless brat getting underfoot."

"That's cold."

Yakov laughed. "It's the truth. He's a pain in the ass. Like Ruthie and Channa and everyone else in this damned place."

When they finished eating, Yakov shook the crumbs from the cloth into his mouth, then handed the cloth back to Stan. "Where'd you get the food?"

"A farm in the country where I used to work. I'm still in contact with the owner."

"A farm boy. I should have known. But you've lost that country innocence, haven't you?"

Stan's brow wrinkled. "What do you mean?"

Yakov stood up, grabbing Stan's chin. His fingers dug in as he turned Stan's head left and right. "So pure, and yet not. Did you think I'd be grateful for the food, for the supplies you've been bringing? You think I'd give you something in return?"

"No, I'm just—" Stan's words cut off as Yakov groped his cock through his trousers.

"Is this what you wanted?" His hand tightened as Stan's prick grew harder, thicker. "Did you think I couldn't tell? You're not as subtle as you think."

"That's not why I—"

"Do you want me to stop?"

"No. Hell, no." Stan leaned in, trying to catch Yakov's mouth with his own, just to feel the stubble on his cheeks, to taste him...

"No." Yakov turned his face away. He tugged Stan's trousers open and shoved his hand inside, his eyes never leaving Stan's face, which grew hot under that stare.

Stan reached down, too, but Yakov turned his body away, pinning Stan's right arm up against the wall. Stan closed his eyes, listening to Yakov's breathing, which grew almost as unsteady as his own.

Yakov kept moving his hand, sliding it up and down the length of Stan's cock, pulling the foreskin almost over the head on each upstroke. "I'll give you what you want," Yakov muttered to the wall, his breath warm on Stan's arm. "Filthy, uncircumcised pig."

"Shut up," Stan said. He tried to pull his hand free from the wall and give Yakov a shove with his body, but Yakov tightened his grip on his wrist. With his free hand, Yakov rubbed over the tip of Stan's cock, smearing the fluid leaking from it, then used it to coat the shaft. He stroked again and again, until Stan's cock was slippery and his heart was about to fly out of his chest.

"Please," Stan croaked, his hips bucking and his legs shaking.

Yakov rubbed his thumb slowly over the head of Stan's cock, as if considering the request, then he began stroking again, long, hard movements, going faster and faster until Stan climaxed, jets of hot semen soaking his trousers. He clung to Yakov, who let go of his wrist in order to cover his mouth, to muffle his rumbling moans.

Yakov kept moving his hand on Stan's cock until the last drop was out, holding him against the wall with his body weight. Then he wiped his hand on Stan's shirt. "Well?"

Stan laughed weakly. "Did something happen? I think my brains left along with that load."

This time Yakov's face didn't go blank, expressionless; he looked almost angry. "Get out." He stepped back, leaving Stan to support his own weight against the wall.

"No."

"Yes. You need to leave."

"Not yet." He reached out and caught Yakov by a coat lapel, then tugged at him. Yakov stayed where he was, but after another yank, he allowed Stan to move him to the wall. Stan then dropped to his knees. He half-expected a punch or a kick, but Yakov didn't move as Stan slowly, carefully unzipped Yakov's trousers and pulled out his cock, which was already hard and leaking. Yakov glared down at him, fists clenched, but his mouth was open and his chest was rapidly rising and falling.

Stan leaned forward and sniffed his way into Yakov's crotch. A hiss of breath from above urged him on. He moved his lips up Yakov's cock, and then took it into his mouth. Holding on to Yakov's thighs, he sucked on the thick prick, sliding his mouth down, down, until the tip hit the back of his throat. In the country, he'd practiced on other farmhands who had been willing to close their eyes and pretend it was a girl's mouth bringing them off. In the city, he found men who were more appreciative of his skills. None of them had been Jews, though, and the lack of foreskin was odd, but not unpleasant.

He continued to do his best, but elicited no reaction from Yakov; no hips surging forward, no hands gripping his hair. Stan decided to risk it. He opened his eyes and looked up. Yakov had his head back against the wall, his teeth bared and clenched, his eyes squeezed shut.

Stan pulled away. "Sorry, did I—" was as far as he got before Yakov grabbed his cock, jerked it a few times, then shot his load right across Stan's face. "Yes," Stan murmured, stroking Yakov's stomach and thighs as Yakov shuddered and then sagged against the wall. When Yakov looked down at Stan, Stan wiped the come off his face and then licked his hand. He then stood up and pulled out the cloth the food had been wrapped in, wiped both of them off and put the cloth back in his pocket.

Yakov was catching his breath, still looking angry, but his eyes were now hooded. Stan waited until Yakov had zipped up his trousers, then nudged him onto the bed. "Get some rest. You look like hell," he lied, making himself leave the room before he did anything stupid—well, even more stupid.

May 10, 1943

"Shoot them!" Stan shouted, scrabbling in his coat pocket for one more bullet.

"No."

"Shoot!"

"Shut up!" Yakov aimed the rifle down at the German troops. "Do you think we have an unlimited supply of ammo? We have to make every shot count!" He went still, staring down the barrel of the gun.

Stan finally found the bullet and loaded it into his pistol. He jumped when Yakov fired.

"Got him! Look at them scatter!" he shouted.

Stan shoved up next to Yakov to peer out the window, to see where the screaming was coming from. Both men ducked at the boom of a grenade going off, then Yakov reloaded to the sound of more screams.

"They're retreating." Stan watched in awe as the German soldiers fled to safety, leaving their wounded in the street. "A couple of shots and one grenade."

"They can't believe Jewish vermin would stick up for themselves, let alone draw German blood while doing it." Yakov spat onto the floor. "That first day, when we saw they could be wounded, killed…that first German body in the street was the dawn after night for every person here."

"Soldiers in apartment windows and alleyways." Stan shook his head. "I always thought wars were fought on battlefields with masses of troops. But I suppose humans love war so much that we're capable of improvising."

"Don't."

"Don't what?" Stan turned around to see Yakov staring at him.

"Don't make jokes."

Frowning, Stan looked down at the street again. "Will they come back?"

"Not if we keep shooting and tossing the occasional Molotov cocktail over the wall."

That's what the fighters did. Every time the Germans approached that day, they were beaten back. After night fell, the fighters went over the wall and stripped the fallen Germans of their weapons, then returned.

Late that night, Stan stood in the doorway to Yakov's room as Yakov sat on the bed, cleaning a rifle. "Why aren't you in a bunker with everyone else?"

"Closer to the action here."

"Closer to the Germans if they manage to get in."

Yakov looked up. "Closer to stopping them if they do. If you don't like it, you can leave."

"Actually, I can't. The sewer entrance we've been using has a tank parked on it. I'm stuck here overnight at least." He leaned against the doorway, trying to look casual. "I was hoping you could find me a place to sleep."

Yakov looked over at Stan, who could practically feel Yakov's eyes traveling down every inch of his body. "Does anyone know about you?" Yakov asked. "That you like to suck cock?"

"There were men before the war, but no one who knows me now."

"How did you know about me?"

Stan stepped into the room, shoving the cleaning kit over so he could sit on the bed. "I wasn't sure. I thought I saw you looking at my ass once. Mostly, I hoped, because you're too damned good-looking to waste on women." He leaned over and kissed Yakov, holding onto his head.

Yakov didn't turn away this time. He let the kiss go on for a few seconds, then broke it off. "Get up."

Stan stood up. At least Yakov hadn't told him to get out.

Yakov stood as well. He put the rifle and cleaning kit under the bed, then pulled Stan's coat off and threw it in the corner. He unbuttoned Stan's shirt, raking his fingernails through blond chest hair, making Stan shiver. When he bent his head to suck on a nipple, one arm tightening around Stan's waist, Stan audibly exhaled.

The shirt hit the floor, then the belt and trousers, until Stan stood naked in the middle of the small, age-beaten room. Yakov walked around him, looking, not speaking. Stan bit his lip to keep from making a smart comment that would get him kicked out.

On his second time around, Yakov came up behind Stan and just stood there, breathing against the back of his neck. Stan shivered again. When Yakov licked him, Stan pushed his bare ass back against the rough cloth of Yakov's trousers, reaching backward for Yakov's hands. But Yakov pulled his hands free, moving up Stan's chest, scraping his fingernails through the hair again before rubbing over hard nipples.

Stan moaned and writhed, trying to turn into Yakov's arms to face him, but Yakov held onto him even more tightly.

"No." And then he let go and stepped away.

"No, wait!" Stan turned around, ready to beg.

Yakov was unbuttoning his shirt. "Turn around and put your hands on the wall." He threw his shirt on the bed and unzipped his trousers. "Unless you're not interested."

Stan slapped his hands onto the wall so hard his palms stung. There was a soft thump as trousers landed on the bed, then Yakov's arms were back around him again, his chest warm against Stan's back, his cock hot and rigid, rubbing between Stan's asscheeks. "Oh god," Stan moaned. He shifted his hips back, but didn't spread his legs. Did Yakov have anything: lotion, oil, petroleum jelly?

Yakov turned away and Stan heard him spit. Damn, this was going to hurt—but Yakov didn't try to penetrate him. Instead, he slipped his cock between Stan's legs, then nudged Stan's feet closer together.

Yakov's cock slid back and forth across that sensitive patch of skin, nudging Stan's balls with every forward thrust. Stan's hands curled into fists against the wall and he tilted his hips for a better angle. When he grabbed his own cock and started stroking, Yakov pulled his hand away. "Keep them on the wall," he muttered.

Stan whined a little, but did as he was told. Yakov would take care of him. He hoped.

Every few thrusts, Yakov stopped to wipe the leaking head of his cock over the area he was probing. Then he started all over again. Soon the spot was slick enough that he didn't need to stop. He held on to Stan's hips and rocked against him.

Stan pushed back against the heat of Yakov's crotch, grinding against the wiry hair there. He could wait for Yakov to take pity on his state and jerk him off; he wasn't going to beg this time—okay, yes, he was. "Yakov," he said, but before he could say "please," Yakov shoved two fingers into Stan's mouth. There was that gun oil smell again, and taste, too. Stan's hips jerked as his cock got even harder. He moaned around the fingers as he sucked on them, then whined when Yakov finally—thank god!—moved his other hand from Stan's hip to his cock.

Yakov didn't move that hand; he let Stan push into it, then pull back, his thighs still tight around Yakov's prick, pushing forward again and again, until Stan was dizzy with sensation. When Stan fell against the wall, panting, so close to the end, Yakov took over. The fingers in Stan's mouth and the hand on his cock moved together, the prick still rubbing beneath his balls, going faster and faster until he heard the grunt, an explosion of breath on his shoulder, then warm wetness spreading between his thighs. He barely kept from biting the fingers in his mouth when he climaxed, finally sagging against the wall. He reached back until he got a hand on Yakov's waist, pulling him tight against his body.

They stood like that for a few minutes until Yakov pulled away—always pulling away. But then he was back with a cold, wet cloth that he tossed to Stan. Stan shivered as he wiped off his stomach and cock, thighs and ass. Yakov rinsed out the cloth in a bowl of water and did his own quick cleanup before getting dressed. "It's late." He put the rifle back together as Stan found his shirt and trousers and also got dressed.

"I thought..." Stan looked at the bed. "But it's really too small. For two, I mean."

"We'll fit. You'd better not snore." Yakov loaded the rifle and a pistol he took from his coat pocket and set them on the floor within easy reach. "You'll have to sleep next to the wall."

"I can do that," Stan told him.

The next morning, Stan yawned and stretched, then looked over at Yakov. "What will you do after the war?"

"Nothing."

"Nothing? Are you wealthy, with no need to work?"

"No."

"Then you must have some plans. You're only, what, twenty-six? Twenty-seven?"

Yakov looked up. "I'm twenty."

"Oh. Sorry, I thought you were older. Than me, I mean."

Yakov scoffed.

"But that just means that you have even more years after this is over."

"It's not going to be over. Not for me."

"But you're holding them off. You can keep doing that—"

"For another few weeks, maybe a month. At some point, we'll run out of ammo or food, then they'll drive us out and put us on the trains. The best I can hope for is a bullet in my head."

"Don't say that."

"It's the truth."

"It doesn't have to be." He rested his chin in the space between Yakov's shoulder and neck. "Some people have gotten out."

"They got out of the ghetto. I don't know what happened to them after that."

"But it's possible."

"I suppose."

"So then, what will you do when this is all over?"

Yakov just shook his head. "You tell me. What will you do? Go back to your cows?"

Stan smiled. "It was a good life. Up with the sun, take care of chores, then a huge breakfast. And in the afternoon, a roll in the hay with the stable hand."

Yakov turned his head to look at him. "Have you ever had any shame?"

"None at all."

"God, I hate it when you make jokes."

"Why? What's wrong with a little humor to bring some light into the darkness? Channa told me that's what you Jews do."

"You're not a Jew. And when did you start chatting with Channa?"

"When she and Ruthie were repairing my uniform. That granddaughter of hers is a whiz with a needle and thread. *They* enjoy my little jokes. But every time I do it, you look like I just read out an obituary."

"Maybe I don't find your little jokes funny."

Stan just looked at him, a lopsided smile pulling at his lips. "I'll figure you out one of these days."

May 14, 1943

"You're good for him," Channa said. "He's not as bitter as he was."

"Good god," Stan said, sputtering and blinking for effect,

making Ruthie laugh. "What on earth was he like before?"

Channa laughed and shook her head. "Ruthie, go fetch some more water."

Ruthie hopped off the stool and left the room. Channa's expression sobered. "I'm not sure how to say this, so I'll just say it. I know you're not spending all your time discussing battle plans."

Stan forced himself to look at her, even though his face was burning up.

She went on. "I don't understand it. I didn't know men could court each other. But I'm glad you are. You make him happy, and I hope he makes you happy, too."

"He does."

"Then I know you have God's blessing. I pray he keeps you both safe."

May 16, 1943

"You come in and out through the sewers."

"Yes."

Yakov tapped his fingers on the windowsill as he looked down into a courtyard, where Ruthie was playing hopscotch with some of the other children.

Stan sighed. "I know what you're thinking. But if I tried to take the children out, we wouldn't get twenty feet past the walls. There are no children left in this part of the city, just the ones in this ghetto. The Germans would know where they came from and they'd take them. The only reason I can get to and from the entrance is the uniform and the forged papers." He moved in front of Yakov, forcing his way into Yakov's line of sight. "If I could get them out, I would. You know that."

"I know." Yakov looked at him. "I know. But I want to see for myself."

"All right."

But before they got halfway down the alleyway, Yakov stopped. "Do you smell that?"

Stan sniffed at the air, then looked up. "Oh no."

A plume of smoke billowed up, curling into the sky over the ghetto.

They turned and ran back toward the shouting, toward the smoke, but Channa stopped them at the entrance to Yakov's building.

"Oh, thank God you're here. I came to find you to tell you not to come back. They're burning everything, driving the people out. It's over."

Yakov swore. "Then I'll take out as many as I can—"

"They'll shoot you on sight. If they see a man like you—young, angry—they'll know you're one of the fighters and they'll kill you on the spot. So you have to get out. Stan, take him with you to the Polish resistance."

"But you and Ruthie, Sollie..."

"They have Ruthie already, and Sollie's dead. He took a grenade. The soldiers surrounded him when he wouldn't raise his hands, then he—" She shook her head and wiped her eyes. Stan swore softly and crossed himself. "He took three Germans with him."

"God almighty." Yakov's voice cracked. "That kid was worth something after all."

"There's nothing more you can do here except die, so go. Now."

"Channa..."

"Go on."

"No! No, no, no, I've got guns, I can distract them while you take the kids out through the sewers or over the wall." He looked up and down the alley, back and forth, his eyes wide, like he was seeing Germans coming around every corner. "I can buy you time. They'll run, they always run, and then it'll—"

She slapped him across the face hard enough to snap his head to the side. "Wake up, Yakov! It's the end. We all know it. You need to go with Stan now. Leave this place." She caught his face, stopping him from shaking his head no. "God has given both of you a multitude of gifts. Don't waste them."

"Come with us," Stan said to Channa.

She shook her head. "I need to stay with Ruthie." She put a hand on each of their heads, closed her eyes and said a few quiet, ancient words. Then she turned and walked toward the dingy hallway.

"Yakov." Stan grasped Yakov's arm. "Come on, we have to go."

"Your memory will be for a blessing," Yakov called after her. She turned and smiled at him, blew him a kiss, and then Stan was dragging him away.

Stan and Yakov climbed out of the sewer and ran. They ran away from the rumble of trucks and jeeps, from the shouts in German and from the sound of hundreds of pairs of worn shoes walking across rubble. Away from the sound of a train grating and shrieking its way into the rail yard.

They ran until they got to parts of the city where people still lived, peering out from behind their curtains. There they walked as if they had every right to be there. Then they ran again, or hid, waiting for danger to pass, until it was dark.

"Let's rest here," Stan said, when they found a house well back from the road. The walls were crumbling, but the roof still covered part of one room. "Tomorrow, I'll go find Tomasz and the others. They'll be glad to have your skills, but I should tell them about you first, before you risk going back into town. I'll see if I can get you some other clothes, because—" He spun around when he heard a high-pitched keening wail, then dropped to his knees next to its source.

Yakov squatted in the rubble of the house, slamming his fists against his head, all the time letting out that ungodly noise. Stan tried to catch his wrists, but Yakov continued to hit himself, pulling at his hair, his mouth open, his face twisted. Every sound out of Yakov's mouth cut into Stan's heart, but he gave up on stopping Yakov from hitting himself and just wrapped his arms around him instead, holding on as tightly as he could. If there were patrols along that road, they would be found in minutes, but he didn't try to quiet Yakov.

Yakov's wails became sobs, shaking his entire body, making his shoulders jerk and his chest heave. He gasped for breath between each sob, his hands gripping Stan's back. "They're dead, they're all dead. I didn't do anything, didn't stop it..."

"You did everything you could."

"It wasn't enough. It wasn't enough."

Stan waited until the sobs became less frequent, until Yakov's breathing became more even. Then he cleared a spot amidst the rubble, lowered Yakov to the floor and lay down behind him, wrapping his arms around him again. After Yakov fell asleep, so did Stan.

"So you have a heart after all." Stan ran the pad of his finger over one thick, dark eyebrow, now just visible in the light of dawn.

Yakov sat up and rubbed his eyes. "I wish I didn't. I wish I could tear it out."

"I'm glad you can't." He sat up as well and touched Yakov's chest, fingertips brushing over the strong heartbeat. Then he stood up. "I'm going to find Tomasz. If everything goes well, I should be back in a few hours, so wait here."

"No."

"But—"

"No!" Yakov scrambled to his feet. "I'll go with you. Or"— he silenced Stan's objection with a look—"I'll go off on my own if you think I'll slow you down. Either way, I'm not going to rot in this ruin waiting for you to come back, when you might not."

Stan gaped at him. "I'm not going to abandon you."

"That's not what I meant."

"Ah." Stan nodded. "You have no faith in my ability to survive."

"No one is lucky all the time."

"No, but I do better than most." He smiled and put a hand on Yakov's cheek. Yakov didn't pull away. "And now that you're with me, you'll have the same luck."

"You think so?"

"I know so. We'll be okay."

"You *don't* know that."

"I *feel* it." Stan leaned in, resting his forehead against Yakov's. "I can't believe the fates would let us meet only to separate us."

"Don't." Yakov took a step back, out of Stan's reach.

"But—"

"I shouldn't have started up with you at all. It's...you're..." He made a disgusted sound. "We shouldn't be doing this," he said, gesturing between the two of them.

Stan raised his eyebrows. "Where did this moral objection suddenly come from?"

"It's not a moral objection." Yakov shook his head. "This... *business* is a distraction we can't afford."

"It's not a distraction." Stan took his hand. "It's a bit of happiness in the middle of a goddamned war. We should be grabbing on to it with both hands."

"Even if it's going to end badly, sooner rather than later?"

"Especially if. But it won't. I told you, we'll be okay." He laughed at Yakov's sour, disbelieving expression. "We will. With my brains and your good looks, there's nothing we can't do."

Yakov rolled his eyes and shook his head again, but he followed Stan out of the house, toward the rising sun.

Upstate New York
June 14, 1962

"Wake up, Yakov, wake up!" Stan shook Yakov gently, then harder, until Yakov woke up with a start.

"What—"

"You were having a nightmare."

Yakov sat up and let out a breath. "Dammit."

Stan rubbed Yakov's back until he felt his heart rate slow down. "Go back to sleep. We've got cows to milk in four hours."

"And a trip into the city after that. Why did you agree to the party?"

"Because Ruthie asked. She threw one for *my* fortieth birthday; you can't escape the same fate."

"My birthday was six months ago."

"And that's when she would have had it if she hadn't just had Channi. Why did *you* offer to take the boys for the whole summer?"

"Because I had a moment of temporary insanity."

Stan curled around Yakov's back, pressing his face into Yakov's hip. "No, because you wanted to give Ruthie and Alan a break. And because you like having those kids around. So do I."

"It's going to be all yelling and feet pounding, dirt and messes and fighting—"

"And you'll love every minute of it." He tugged down the waistband of Yakov's pajama bottoms and sucked on his hip. "You know, this is the last night we won't have to be quiet for the next couple of months."

Yakov pushed his fingers into Stan's hair, rubbing his scalp. "I won't be able to get back to sleep now anyway." He pulled off his pajamas and threw them onto the nightstand, while Stan did the same. Then Yakov pressed Stan down on the bed and lay on top of him, Stan's few extra pounds providing the padding for Yakov's still-lean frame. They shared a long kiss, their tongues mapping mouths they'd known for twenty years. No more furtive groping when they had a few minutes away from their fellow resistance fighters, no more of the necessary celibacy of the refugee centers after the war. In their own home, their own bed, they could take their time: a slow, smooth slide of skin against skin, tongue against tongue, hands clasping, releasing, holding tight; Stan's gasp when Yakov took him in his mouth; his cry when Yakov drained him.

When Stan started to move down Yakov's body, Yakov stopped him. He lay down next to Stan and kissed him again, then began a slow rocking against his hip, stroking a hand across Stan's furry chest and stomach. Stan did the same to him, returning the kiss until Yakov shifted to make his way down Stan's jaw to his neck. He bit down gently, then scraped his teeth across the skin there. Stan growled in pleasure, and that was enough to make Yakov lose himself, shaking as he came. "I love you so much," he panted into Stan's hair.

Stan touched his cheek, gave him a brief, hard kiss on the mouth. "Say that to me when you haven't just come," he murmured, smiling against Yakov's mouth.

Yakov got out of bed and brought back a damp washcloth to clean them both up. He then climbed back into bed, spooning up behind Stan and throwing an arm over his waist. "I love you so much."

Stan wriggled back against him. "Hard to believe you're the same man who wouldn't laugh at my jokes."

"I had to force myself not to. I didn't want to start liking you. It would have made me too sad when you got killed."

"But I didn't get killed, did I?"

"So you want me to retroactively laugh at every joke you ever told?"

"That would be a good start."

Yakov pinched Stan's ass, making him snicker. "How did you know, though? That we'd be all right? That we'd survive?"

Stan put his arm over Yakov's and pulled it in tight to his stomach. "I didn't. I just hoped. Even when I got shot, when you got caught in that building that collapsed, I didn't know. But I hoped. Because I loved you too much for either of us to die just when you were starting to tolerate me."

"Tolerate you. Sure." Yakov snorted. "You were irresistible and you knew it. Middle of a damned war, and I was taking my clothes off for you."

"You still do that."

"You're still irresistible." Yakov pressed his lips to the back of Stan's neck. After a few seconds, they were both asleep again.

A TIME FOR THIEVES

Eric Del Carlo

A damned quest was the last thing Keane had expected. A mere two weeks prior, he had sat rotting in the slimy stone hollow of his lord's most despicable dungeon, where conditions were so appalling the guards didn't even bother torturing you. Now, one conditional reprieve later, Keane had set out with a band of semi-deranged misfits and hot-tempered killers, all assembled for this most impossible assignment: raid the treasure room of a fellow lord's neighboring castle.

Britannia was an island of madmen. It would be better to have the damned Romans back, like in Keane's grandfather's time.

The lord under whom Keane lived wanted more wealth to add to his already gluttonous riches. *So be it,* Keane had thought when the offer to join the quest had come. He was a skilled thief, although those talents hadn't kept him from getting caught on his last job. Actually, it had been his partner who had betrayed him. Keane should have listened to his instincts before that adventure: never trust another thief. For three months in the suffocating horror of the dungeon, he had contemplated his error. And what had come of that? Here he was, *again* working with criminals.

On this perilous journey, their company had slogged across moors, fought cold and disease, even battled a party of pirates who had tried to board their boat as the group made the crossing of a lake. Keane found it strange how quickly the relief of open sky and the illusion of freedom had given way to the grumbling discomfort of crossing vast stretches of hostile territory. More than once he'd had to stop himself from thinking fondly of his foul little cell, where no one demanded anything of him.

But this freedom was indeed illusion. Neither he nor any of the other temporarily released prisoners assembled for this mission were free. Four members of the king's elite guard had come along on this mad venture, and it was the duty of these expert soldiers to keep any of the criminals from trying to sneak off. Already they had caught one and had made an example of him, hacking off his head while all were made to watch.

"Get to sleep, you lot," said the captain of the guard, surveying the little camp they'd erected for the night. "Tomorrow we'll be in sight of the castle keep; then the fun really begins." The captain grinned maliciously.

Keane, huddled on his bedroll under the stars, felt his desperation rising. The company was expected to infiltrate that forbidding keep, to use all their talents to bring out as much gold and jewels as they could. A job of thievery. But, very likely, an impossible one. The castle was too secure, the rival lord too cunning, the treasure room too well guarded.

He fought to sleep, which was a losing struggle. It had always been thus for Keane on the night before a job, even when he was a boy. Now he was a man, firm of body, his dark hair tangled and long. He didn't wish to return to the dungeon, but he doubted he would survive this adventure.

Above, the sky blackened as clouds moved in, robbing the

stars themselves. Around him, Keane heard the snores and murmurs of his fellows, evidently finding sleep more easily than he. The guards were not anywhere in sight, though by now the darkness was nearly total.

Sweat pasted his leather shirt to his muscled chest. His blood pounded in his ears. Slowly he rose onto an elbow, looking over the camp. Just enough moonlight bled through the cloud cover to show him the mounds of the sleepers. Their guards were watching this small encampment in the field. There were four of the elite. If only one was assigned as lookout, maybe he would not be paying too close attention. Guards nodded off. It happened, even to experienced soldiers.

Keane let the meager shred of hope overtake him. As if obeying another's will, he slipped from his bedroll onto a thief's silent feet. Step by step he moved, crouching, imagining himself a shadow, something that couldn't even disturb the air. He went soundlessly, without even the tiniest crunch of a muffled footfall. He threaded the scattered sleepers, alerting no one.

Escape. True freedom. He would simply disappear, find some other place to live his life, away from his lord's influence. Perhaps he would even give up thieving! The thought made him energetic, almost giddy, and for several instants after entertaining it, he almost believed he could do it. Take up some legitimate trade, become respectable—

"Nice night for a stroll."

It was the finest of whispers, one that somehow cut through the dark, aimed straight for Keane. He froze, well beyond the camp's edge by now. He realized he had let himself think ahead, past the moment. Hope was dangerous. A thief should know better.

But it had been foolish—*ludicrous*—to imagine he could get away. Now he had to deal with the consequences. The first, best way to do that was to lie.

Still not seeing the member of the guard who'd spoken in the darkness, Keane said, "Got to take a piss. Don't want to do it in the camp."

"You're far enough," said the voice, calm, measured— perhaps a little amused? "Go where you're standing."

Deception was a staple of the thief's trade, as Keane well knew. The only problem with lying was getting caught at it. Though his bladder was quite empty, he undid his breeches, hoping he could produce a few errant drops.

Straining, feet splayed and himself in hand, Keane felt fear. He had seen the hopeful escapee executed a few days ago. And there was that damned word again: *hope*. Still struggling to urinate, he now saw the ghost of movement on his left. A figure was drifting into view from the high grass at the field's brim. The guard was allowing himself to be seen, Keane knew. How quietly he glided, the long fronds not even whispering against the long, taut legs.

This soldier was not the captain, of course, who wouldn't give himself the duty of guarding the camp. Rather, the figure was the strangest looking one in the bunch, with wan skin and delicate features. Hair as long as Keane's own spilled onto tight high shoulders, the color a downy white where Keane's was consumingly black. Even the man's eyes were odd, a pink that was unnatural. He had probably been assigned to this detail to keep the paroled prisoners frightened. Some among the company thought him a witch.

"Well, if you're not going to have that piss," the guard murmured, the soft trill of amusement now definitely present in that voice, "then what did you plan to do with...*that*?"

Keane still had himself in hand. But now, it seemed, his cock had begun to thicken. It was due to the presence of this person. Keane realized that from almost this journey's outset he had been eyeing the faerie-like man, entertaining secret lascivious thoughts. His bizarre appearance intrigued and aroused Keane. Surely a quest was no place for romance, but the mounting tension of this perilous venture had gotten to him and was at last expressing itself as outright lust.

He met the guard's eyes. Slowly, deliberately, he played his fingers up and down his swelling shaft. The night, though overcast, was warm. He asked, "What would you have me do?"

White teeth appeared between fine lips as the male grinned at him. Keane smiled back. His excitement rose.

"Come here," came the whisper, which was huskier now.

Keane spared a glance behind, but nothing stirred in the camp. Surely this soldier was the only one on guard duty; the others needed to sleep. Keane crept forward, leaving his breeches unfastened, his still hardening manhood dangling. This was better than feeling afraid, he decided. His flesh tingled in anticipation.

He slipped in among the high grass, the soft blades shushing around his body. The guard waited for him. He wore the royal uniform, now quite stained by travel. His sword belt hung about a narrow waist. The weapon in its sheath had a dark grooved hilt, a lone pale stone set into the pommel.

Keane found his breath coming raggedly. The elfin skin and hair seemed to emit their own soft light. He was so beautiful in his unnaturalness, Keane thought, seeing clearly the planes of his features, the point of his chin, the glimmering pinkness of his eyes.

"What," Keane asked again, now standing close to the guard, "would you have me do?" With his fist he was pumping his fully erect cock in earnest now. If need be, he would bring himself to climax for this soldier's amusement. He would, he realized suddenly, do anything that was asked of him. The rising wave of lust was powerful, overwhelming. As desperate as he had been to escape a few moments ago, he was now that bent on pleasing this individual.

The pink eyes were steady, but Keane saw the glint of a deep heat there. The guard said, "Take off those clothes."

The dark grass stood up about their shoulders. Quickly, Keane dropped his breeches, stepping out of his boots. The air felt good on his sore feet. He wrestled the leather shirt up over his head. A gentle night breeze stirred the field, and expectant gooseflesh stood out all over his body. His cock throbbed now, a dewdrop glistening at its tip. Normally, he didn't conduct his sexual activities in this manner. But he'd been three months in that dungeon's fetid bowels, and the stress of this quest had transformed his usual carnal responses out of all proportion.

That or he just really wanted to fuck this lovely white-haired male.

The guard was still grinning. With one hand he loosened a catch on his uniform trousers and reached within. His other hand rested atop his sword's pommel. Keane understood the gesture; they were about to become lovers, but the lord's soldier would not trust him. That suited Keane. He didn't want to be trusted.

"Take this in your mouth," the soldier said, drawing a pale, stiffening cock into the faint moonglow. But Keane, not needing the prompt, was already kneeling. A great hunger took hold of him. It was better than hope; it was something he could immediately satisfy.

His bare knees sank among the grass and he beheld the glorious cock at eye level. Its creamy length was offset by the rosy blush of the swollen head. Hand shaking slightly, Keane took gentle hold of the base of the cock, feeling the testicles stir against his knuckles. He traced the underside vein with the nail of his thumb, and the member twitched. Keane opened his mouth, let his head slide forward.

His lips enclosed the cockhead, and the familiar masculine flavor spread through his mouth. It was like the shock of hot food after a strenuous day. He felt his whole body snap, naked limbs rustling the fronds, his own cock quivering, dripping another bead of anticipatory fluid.

Somewhere above, a soft grunt of pleasure sounded. The thick fabric of the uniform trousers brushed Keane's bare skin as he sank the ring of his lips farther along the straining shaft. The guard had surged into full hardness. Keane swallowed him fearlessly, the crown of the cock now slipping into his throat. He sank his cheeks around the intruding staff, his tongue exploring the smaller erratic veins that lined it.

Keane worked his mouth down to the cock's hilt until his forehead pressed against the taut, flat belly. Anybody could do as the soldier had instructed—take a cock in one's mouth—but it required someone who genuinely relished the act to devour one so completely. Keane felt the strange frantic urge to prove himself to this male.

His mouth rose and fell now, slowly at first, demonstrating his prowess—showing off. With each plunge, he took the whole of the rigid staff. He shifted his hand to softly cup the guard's balls now, fondling the pouch.

After a moment, Keane picked up the tempo. The scent and taste of this luscious cock now suffused him, as if its innate masculinity were pouring through every part of his being. He closed his eyes. He let his neck muscles take over. He heard the quiet tight slurps of his mouth. He anticipated the inevitable jetting of this organ and wanted that ultimate flavor more than anything just now.

The guard was shifting his stance, fidgeting about. Fabric rustled. It took Keane another moment before he opened his eyes, looking up through a kind of carnal haze to see that his lover had somehow managed to shed his clothing without breaking contact with Keane's mouth. Pale flesh glimmered, the body lean and firm. He retained only the sword belt, one hand still caressing the pale stone of the pommel.

With his other hand, he grasped Keane's dark tangled hair. He started to thrust himself against every downward plummet of Keane's mouth. Soon, they fell into a productive rhythm.

Keane accepted each lunge, his throat already delightfully raw. Somehow, they were managing to stay quiet, their movements and moans no louder than the stray breezes grazing the night.

By now, their congress was as frenzied and focused as the plunges of an oar into the lake. Keane's mouth rode the guard's cock, lips sealed around the pulsing shaft. The pale-skinned man thrust at Keane's face, long fingers clutching his dark mass of hair. Keane felt the balls in his grip tighten, and an instant later the hot salty fluid started to flow.

Eagerly, he swallowed every spurt, the heady taste of male rapture inundating him. As he often had in the past, Keane felt a keen pride at what he had accomplished. This joy belonged to him. He had created it for this other person. His mouth had worked the simple sexual miracle.

The guard's grip eased and the fingers slid from his hair. The soldier retreated a half step, slipping his slowly wilting cock from Keane's lips. Keane rocked back on his haunches, his own manhood still painfully hard. He savored the guard's flavor, catching a stray drip on his fingertip that had found its way from the corner of his mouth. He looked up, smiling.

The pale man was such a beauty. Here he stood, naked but for the sheathed sword and the belt cinching his slim waist, like some mad erotic dream of a warrior. His white flesh still seemed to glow.

Keane continued looking up dreamily at the male he had just fellated. With a suddenness of movement that didn't even allow time to blink, the soldier swept his sword from its scabbard with barely a rasp of steel. Abruptly, the long blade gleamed in the night. The elf-like male held the weapon with a perfect control. The metal length didn't waver as he pointed it toward Keane.

He is going to behead me, Keane thought, the realization so immediate and dire that he could attach no emotion to it. But he was wrong. For one, the member of the lord's elite could have taken off his head in the same motion as the drawing of the sword. For another, the man told him, "You're going to fuck my ass, boy. But I have to make certain you don't run away while I'm on hands and knees. Try it, and I'll swivel round and gut you."

With that, the guard turned away, kneeling in the high grass. He laid the unsheathed sword on the ground, near his fighting hand, and offered up his sculpted, pale ass.

It was still like something culled from a dream. Keane moved in behind the man. He looked down in dazed wonder at what was being presented to him. His own body streamed with need, his nerves twanging and buzzing. Almost reverently, he laid his hands to the perfect backside, cupping the twin hemispheres. Keane's cock quivered, ready to perform the ultimate impalement.

But practical matters first. With his tongue still slick with the guard's semen, he lowered his head and lapped at the pearly hole, spearing inside, wetting the entrance. The soldier, on hands and knees, wriggled a little, already pushing back against the intrusion, driving Keane's tongue deeper inside.

He spent perhaps a moment longer than necessary slurping at the sweet entryway. Then he rose and fitted the distended head of his cock to the pale ass. The firm but pliant ring took him in, spreading over Keane's cockhead, swallowing him, drawing him farther inside the waiting canal. He eased in, thrilling at the enclosing heat. He set his hands to the narrow hips, fingers slipping over the bones as neatly as a hand would fit the grooves on the soldier's sword handle.

Keane was still easing inside when the guard's white-haired head turned and pink eyes pierced him. Fine lips peeled back from his teeth. "Hurry, boy!" he whispered fiercely. "How much time do you think we've got?"

It snapped Keane back to the reality of this incredible situation. They were two males—enemies, essentially—grabbing a fast fuck in the grass while one of them was on duty and the other was supposed to be sleeping. If the other members of the guard happened upon this scene, *God*, if the captain came along—

But they were all, hopefully, asleep in their own little encampment adjacent to this field. Still, there was no time to waste. Keane set about plunging his cock into his lover's ass. The grip of the channel was exquisite. He watched his straining length disappear again and again into the willing hole. The belt and empty scabbard still hung about the soldier's boyishly trim waist. He had turned his head away, his long colorless hair spilling across his high shoulders. His pronounced spine flexed among the flat muscles along his back. His ass shivered as Keane thrust into him.

Again, he increased the tempo. The soft pats of Keane's balls against the soldier's backside quickened. Pleasure welled through him, its intensity almost painful. The improbability of this scenario only added to the excitement. Maybe the last thing he'd expected on this quest was the chance to fuck one of the guards—and this one in particular, this lovely male with the thin, pale form.

The guard's head whipped from side to side, all the muscles of his body clenching. Keane felt that tightness. He realized that the man was jetting a second time on the ground. In that same instant, he felt his own first wrenches of joy. Hot fluid erupted, seeding the soldier's ass. The bliss clawed across Keane's bare body, and he had to clamp his teeth together to keep from crying out.

All around, the dim night flared for him, lighting up with a radiant paleness, as though his lover's strange flesh had, for that moment, become his whole world.

He did not try to escape. The guard, therefore, didn't need to gut him with his sword. The two men remained still a moment, and then disengaged. They stood and dressed, their movements silent. Nothing stirred from the camp but the snores and mutters of exhausted travelers.

Before he returned to his bedroll, Keane put a hand to the guard's arm and asked, "What is your name?"

He might not have answered. The sex might have been their only intimacy, and once done, the soldier could have regarded him with contempt, as if the act had been meaningless. But the eyes beheld him, and there was a warmth within the pink depths. "I am Digby," he said.

Keane kissed him, gently, on the lips. Then he returned to the camp and Digby resumed his watching. Tomorrow, so the captain had said, they would come within sight of the keep of the rival lord. Also within sight would be the end of this crazy quest, which would no doubt mean death for most, if not all, of this criminal company.

Air burning in his lungs, the pain searing his muscular chest, Keane staggered onward. He was a creature of exhausted instinct by now, dripping with sweat and blood. His sight was awash with frantic white motes, and lifting each foot for another forward stride required a titanic effort.

Yet, he still clutched the prize. His hands remained locked about the handle of the treasure box.

They had succeeded. Keane had reached the special chamber at the end of a labyrinth of corridors, all of it tremendously disorienting. He had slain the final guardian, snapping the man's neck. The rival lord's soldiers were good ones, but they weren't prepared, it seemed, for the work of professional thieves. The band of criminals had studied the castle from without for a full day, over the protests of the elite guard's captain. He had wanted them to have at the place immediately, probably with an eye toward getting this impossible task over with.

Instead of failure, however, they'd achieved success! The giddy thought swirled in Keane's head as he stumbled on, feet falling on rocky terrain now. He had somehow gotten past the outer wall.

With the weighty chest in his hands, he took another fumbling step, then his nerveless legs simply gave out. He dropped heavily, falling onto his side. He would not let go of the ornate metal box, no matter what, not even if the members of the rival lord's army—any that were still alive—came in pursuit. There had been more treasure in that secret room, but this was the best of it. He had seen inside the chest, the coins of every size, jewels in a sea of colors.

He was still lying there, gradually growing aware of the sunlight and the sounds of birds, when he heard the crunch of footsteps on the turf. The passageways of the keep had run with blood. His fellow thieves had done their jobs, whether or not any of them had lived. Their reprieve from their penal sentences had always been conditional: they had to succeed at this quest and they had to survive it. Maybe none of them had done that. Maybe only Keane. And now someone was coming.

"Somehow, I knew it would be you."

Keane's eyes were open, but he was only now starting to see again.

"Digby…"

The pale man knelt beside him, his sword undrawn. He reached out, but not to take the treasure box; rather, to smooth back the damp hair from Keane's brow. The soldier offered a tender smile.

"Are you injured?"

"I…" Keane drew several breaths. The burning had eased somewhat. "I don't know."

"I think you would know," Digby said. Strong hands cradled Keane's shoulders, bringing him up into a sitting position. Keane blinked dazedly. The smoking keep stood some distance away across a swath of stony ground. No one from their company was nearby, nor any of the rival soldiers.

Neither were any others of Keane's lord's guard within view. Had they been sent to look for survivors? Would the captain even bother what that, Keane wondered?

"Now we can go," Digby said. He was holding Keane, rocking him gently. His lips brushed Keane's dark hair.

"Go?" Keane heard himself ask inanely. Yes, of course. Go back over the lake and across the moors. Take the greedy lord his prize.

"Yes," said Digby, still embracing him. He had made no move to take the chest. Something was wrong with his uniform, Keane slowly realized. The insignia had been removed. He couldn't make sense of that. Digby said, "You and I. The captain put me on to preparing the day's rations for him and the other two. So prepare them I did. They'll sleep for...oh, quite a while, if the apothecary was even remotely right. Plenty of time for us to get away."

Keane's mind could barely begin to grasp what the soldier was saying. He managed to ask, "Go where, Digby?"

The white-fleshed male smiled down at him. "Wherever we like. There are other lands. Two enterprising fellows like us ought to be able to make their way. And we'll have plenty to spend as we go." He nodded at the elaborately molded box.

The formerly loyal member of the lord's guard—now himself a thief, evidently—finally reached to the treasure chest and opened it. Keane had already seen to the lock. Digby grinned at the bright wonders within. Pink eyes aflame, he said, "It is our future. It's beautiful, Keane. Very beautiful." The light in his eyes formed into a single tear, which spilled onto Keane's cheek. Keane smiled up at his lover.

Digby helped him onto his feet, and together they headed off to the south, away from everything they had ever known.

MORE USE ALIVE

Jonathan Asche

The Roman leaned over the Gothic warrior's shoulder, his beard brushing the side of his captor's neck. "How could you betray me?" he growled.

Gerung chuckled. "Were it not for me, you would end up with an arrow in your throat, just like your horse."

He then kicked his own horse and the animal broke into a trot. Though now a prisoner, the Roman—Lucanus, son of Trajan Papirius, as he had haughtily informed the other men of Gerung's tribe—shared Gerung's saddle, over the protests of Asbad, the more ruthless of Gerung's tribesmen. "A prisoner should be forced to walk!"

"The night grows long," said Valimer, the chieftain and Gerung's father. "You want to make it even longer?"

Leather straps bound Lucanus's wrists and he had to struggle to keep his balance astride the horse as it moved deeper into the forest. He was nude—"A prisoner has no right to dress as a nobleman," Gerung had said as he tore off Lucanus's tunic—and felt the cool night air against the broad expanse of his bare back and the heat of his captor's body warming his front. The rhythmic bouncing of the horse created a pleasurable friction and caused Lucanus's cock to swell against Gerung's buttocks. The *Vesi* warrior made no comment, but clucked his tongue to urge his horse to move faster.

The tribe's camp was hidden in the hills, shielded by trees. Most of the members were in their tents, though a few, hearing the return of the warriors, came out to learn the fate of the Roman who had been spotted outside their camp an hour earlier. They laughed when they saw the naked man riding on the back of Gerung's horse. Lucanus looked past them, ignoring their jeers.

Gerung volunteered to keep the prisoner in his tent. His father at first protested, arguing that Lucanus should be put in a tent with some of the other soldiers, but Gerung persevered.

"Who would you trust to not mistreat him? Asbad?" Gerung had asked.

Inside his tent, Gerung lit a lantern. Lucanus sat in the corner, the lantern's dim glow highlighting the ridges of his muscular body, making him seem more a bronze statue than a man.

The Roman was seething. "I should tell them everything," he hissed.

Gerung's smile was patronizing. "They would not believe you."

Lucanus was undeterred. "Take me to your father. I will tell him."

Gerung took off his helmet and undid his belt. "Let him enjoy his wine. We can make your story more interesting in the meantime."

A scowl remained on Lucanus's handsome face a moment longer, replaced with a smile when he realized what Gerung was inferring. "Then should you not untie me?"

Gerung peeled off his rough woolen tunic, revealing a tautly muscled torso. "Later, perhaps," he said, sweeping his long tawny hair away from his face.

The young warrior knelt in front of his prisoner and leaned

in, softly kissing Lucanus's plush lips. He pulled away. The two men looked into each other's eyes and traded smiles. Gerung kissed the Roman again, harder this time. Lucanus responded with equal force.

Gerung reluctantly pulled his mouth away. A glistening thread of their spit bridged their lips, breaking when Gerung spoke. "You understand why I convinced my father to take you prisoner. Asbad would have killed you otherwise."

"I do see the advantages. If only my horse was spared."

"Even if it had lived, you would not be leaving with it. Father is no doubt angry at Asbad for wasting such a fine beast."

"So then, when will I be leaving?" Lucanus asked.

A mischievous glint appeared in Gerung's eyes. "It doesn't appear you want to," he said, reaching for Lucanus's stiffening cock. "In fact, I may never want to let you go."

Lucanus chuckled softly as Gerung stroked him. "You can hold me as long as you like if it's my cock you are holding," he purred, tilting back his head and lowering his eyelids.

Was it only two days earlier that Lucanus had first spotted Gerung at the stream near the road to Perusia? It seemed a lifetime ago when he saw the young barbarian through the trees, splashing around in the water. Lucanus had slowed his approach, his caution not so much because he recognized the other man as belonging to the enemies of the Empire but because Lucanus wanted the freedom to admire him. He had always believed the people of the Gothic tribes to be dirty and ugly, but this one was as beautiful as any Roman, with taut muscles and pale skin. Even from a distance, Lucanus could see Gerung had a handsome face, his dark blond beard failing to mask its youth. The boyish face and manly body—to say nothing of his godlike cock—had so transfixed Lucanus that when the barbarian climbed onto the shore, he did not consider that it might be a sign of trouble.

The warm, wet caress of Gerung's tongue on his cock brought Lucanus out of his reverie. A groan escaped his lips. Gerung took his mouth away from Lucanus's throbbing prick long enough to look up at him and smile.

"You best be quiet," he said, his hand gently stroking his captive's shaft. "The others might think I'm torturing you."

"But you are torturing me," Lucanus panted.

"I've only just begun." Gerung returned his mouth to the Roman's stiff prick, swallowing it whole.

Gerung had a talented tongue. Lucanus learned this the day he first met him, but only after he learned Gerung was quick with a blade, the young *Vesi* appearing suddenly, naked and dripping wet, beside Lucanus's horse.

Lucanus told him he only wanted to let his horse drink, but when Lucanus dismounted, it became plain that the Roman wasn't just wanting to slake his horse's thirst.

The naked barbarian laughed. "Your sword is almost as hard as mine," he said in stilted Latin, lightly tapping the jutting protuberance at the front of Lucanus's tunic with the flat side of his sword, "but mine is sharper."

The steel blade against his cock simultaneously excited and terrified the Roman. He laughed nervously and then genuinely.

"We should be equally matched," he said and pointed at the other man's still rising cock.

Gerung blushed, and then lowered his sword. He and Lucanus exchanged names, but not any details about where they came from or their stations. They knew all they needed to know: they were enemies, yet they were drawn to each other.

Still, Gerung was suspicious when Lucanus stepped toward him. He raised his sword defensively. Lucanus kissed him and Gerung's sword fell to the ground, all before Gerung sank to his knees.

Now, in Gerung's tent, the barbarian was sucking ravenously on Lucanus's cock. His long, unruly hair fell across the Roman's muscular thighs, covering Lucanus's lap. Were his hands free, Lucanus would have pulled back Gerung's hair and watched his cock disappear into the young man's hungry mouth. With his hands restricted, he could only squirm and tremble as the pleasure became greater and greater, until it was practically unbearable.

"*Eia!*" he cried, moments before his cock erupted in Gerung's mouth.

The young *Vesi* was as hungry now as he was the first day he wrapped his mouth around Lucanus's cock, gulping down his hot seed and refusing to release the Roman's cock from his mouth until he had swallowed every drop. Deep groans burst from Lucanus's mouth, followed by a quick intake of breath, as if he were trying to suck the noises he made back into his lungs. Only when Gerung had drained his balls and pulled his mouth away from his captive's cock did Lucanus's groaning finally cease.

Gerung sat up, grinning impishly. His wet lips glistened in the dim lantern light. His eyes danced.

"If only I could always eat as well," he teased before leaning in to kiss Lucanus.

The taste of his seed on Gerung's tongue and the warmth of the barbarian's lips sent a tingle up Lucanus's spine. "Please untie me," he whispered. "It truly is torture not being able to put my hands on you."

"We should all be so lucky to be so tortured," Gerung said pointedly before rising to his feet. The front of his dusty brown trousers bulged obscenely, enticingly. Gerung untied the drawstring of his *braccae* and slowly pushed them down his hips.

Lucanus licked his lips reflexively upon seeing the Gothic warrior's cock spring free. Though Lucanus was the more generously endowed of the two men, Gerung's prick was, to the Roman's eyes, near perfect, from the uniform thickness of its shaft to the voluptuous curve of the glans.

Gerung stepped out of his pants and flung them aside. Lucanus's cock jumped, revived by the sight of the naked *Vesi* walking toward him.

"If you cannot touch me with your hands, your mouth will have to," Gerung said, stopping in front of the Roman.

The tip of Gerung's prick brushed across Lucanus's forehead, leaving behind a silvery trail of his juices. Lucanus inhaled the woodsy musk wafting from his lover's succulent, pendulous balls.

Lucanus's lips trembled. In his limited experience, with slaves and the young men who sold themselves in town, Lucanus had resisted sucking cock. He had refused on the day of that first meeting too, claiming it was a weakness to taste another man's meat.

"Weakness or fear?" Gerung challenged playfully. "I thought you Romans were afraid of nothing."

Lucanus had tried to steel himself against the barbarian's teasing that day, but relented. Though it was temptation, not Gerung's taunting, that made him finally put his mouth on another man's cock. He did so hesitantly at first—brushing his lips across the tip, tentatively running his tongue around the corona—before sliding the stiff organ into his mouth. Lucanus soon came to the conclusion that if sucking cock was a form of surrender then he would gladly surrender to Gerung.

"I can still see you that day of our first meeting, jerking away at the first burst from my cock." Gerung chuckled softly as Lucanus's mouth closed over his throbbing manhood. "Looked like someone threw a pail of milk in your face."

Lucanus pulled his mouth away from his captor's cock. "I should think by now you wouldn't have enough in your balls to fill a pail."

"No, only enough to fill your mouth," Gerung grunted before stuffing his cock back between Lucanus's moist lips.

The tent was quickly filled with Gerung's soft moans of pleasure as Lucanus's tongue circled the swollen crown of his cock. Lucanus struggled against the leather straps binding his wrists, wishing he were free to move his hands over the other man's body, to feel the firm ridges of muscle beneath smooth skin, the curve of his buttocks, the softness of his hair. Yet, the restriction of his hands also heightened his arousal. His cock was stiff and pulsing, as if Lucanus were experiencing the young warrior's body for the first time.

Gerung thrust his hips, pushing his cock deeper down the Roman's throat. Lucanus rolled his eyes up to see Gerung smiling down at him.

"Maybe I've tortured you enough," he said, combing his fingers through Lucanus's thick hair. Then he pulled his cock from Lucanus's mouth, laughing when the Roman leaned forward to recapture it with his lips.

The *Vesi* picked up a knife. A vague feeling of unease crept into Lucanus's chest as Gerung approached him with the blade, though he knew he had nothing to fear. Still, Gerung had only been his lover for a few days; Gerung's people had been enemies of the Empire for a lifetime.

Gerung crouched behind Lucanus and cut the straps from his wrists and tossed the knife aside. "Will you now run or will you fuck me instead?"

Panting, Lucanus turned and seized Gerung in his arms, pulling the other man to him. They kissed, at first affectionately and then deeply, lustfully, falling into a heap on the grassy floor of the tent. Lucanus's hands glided down Gerung's back, finding purchase on the twin hillocks of the barbarian's ass.

"I would only run if you were running with me," Lucanus said, kneading Gerung's firm buttocks, "and only *after* I fucked you."

Gerung growled, grinding his body atop Lucanus's. Their cocks rubbed together, sparking a heat that was hotter than any fire. Gerung raised his hips and reached for Lucancus's engorged cock, pulling it forward until it was between his thighs and pressed between his asscheeks. He rolled his hips, massaging Lacanus's shaft with his butt.

Overcome with lust, Lucanus grabbed a fistful of Gerung's

hair and pulled it, like the reins of a horse, raising the warrior's face so he could kiss him again. The kiss was harder this time, and Lucanus could feel Gerung trembling on top of him.

They pulled their mouths apart, both men gasping for breath. Lucanus slipped his fingers into Gerung's mouth. Gerung sucked on them as adeptly as he had sucked on Lucanus's prick. When the Roman withdrew his fingers, they were dripping with the barbarian's spit.

His hand went immediately to Gerung's ass, wet fingers sliding between Gerung's buttocks. His fingers easily entered, probed.

Gerung closed his eyes and let out a low groan. He raised his ass and leaned into the Roman's fingers, squeezing the digits with the muscles of his ass. Gerung muttered something in his native tongue, the harshness of his language softened by his low, breathy voice.

A moment later, Gerung sat up. He spit in his palm and wrapped his hand around Lucanus's cock, making it slick. Slowly, he lowered himself onto Lucanus, pausing at the moment of penetration, closing his eyes and inhaling deeply. On their first encounter, Gerung was hesitant at allowing Lucanus to fuck him, claiming he was too big.

It was now Lucanus's turn to do the teasing. "The brave barbarian is not afraid of being pierced by a sword, but withers at a cock?"

Gerung responded with a smile—a smile that became a grimace as Lucanus's cock disappeared inside of him. A moment later, the smile returned, joined with a sigh.

The full length of Lucanus's member was deep inside him. The barbarian's pulsing, dripping cock showed his pleasure to great effect. The sight of it made Lucanus's prick throb inside. Slaves and prostitutes were merely acquiescent; Gerung actually took joy in getting fucked.

Gently undulating his hips, Gerung closed his eyes and

uttered more unintelligible words in his own language. Lucanus gripped his thighs and thrust into him, shuddering as a warm, tingling sensation buzzed through his body.

The captor leaned down to kiss his prisoner. The Roman's strong arms encircled his body, holding Gerung against his broad chest. *"Tu es pulcher,"* he whispered in Gerung's ear, driving his cock deep into the young man's ass. Gerung's response to being told he was beautiful was a terse grunt.

Lucanus dug his fingers into Gerung's ass and rammed his cock even deeper. Gerung groaned and rolled his hips, his body twisting and sliding against Lucanus's Herculean form. He lapsed back into his native language, and Lucanus thought he heard the *Vesi's* word for love, but it could just as easily have been an obscenity. Regardless, it was poetry once uttered by Gerung.

The two men writhed on the tent's floor, their sweaty bodies shimmering in the amber lantern light. Their breathing became heavy, their movements more forceful, almost violent. They spoke in grunts and groans, and then sudden cries of ecstasy that were silenced with long, probing kisses. At last, Gerung's cock spurted onto Lucanus's taut belly, his seed forming a sticky seal between their bodies.

Lucanus's body quivered. Pressing his hands into Gerung's back, he made an anguished, gasping cry as his own seed gushed into the barbarian's guts.

They lay together, still joined and pleasantly spent. Lucanus sighed and stroked Gerung's hair. This was a new experience, this lying together and luxuriating in the afterglow instead of hastily disappearing into the night. Lucanus would, at those times, return to Perusia to tell his father he had been riding; Gerung, in turn, would try to kill a rabbit or bird, claiming to his father that he had been away hunting the whole time.

That night, for the first time, the barbarian and the Roman— the captor and the captive—slept in each other's arms.

A man's shouting woke them at sunrise. Lucanus opened his eyes, then immediately sat up, startled to discover the man was in the tent. It was Asbad, the warrior who discovered him in the forest on his way to meet Gerung, the same one who shot an arrow through his horse's neck. Gerung was up, struggling to get into his *braccae*, yelling at Asbad to get out.

"Romans," he spat, leveling his hateful glare at Lucanus. "They're just over the hillside."

Gerung's father, Valimer, entered the tent at that moment, shouting orders. He also cast an angry gaze at their prisoner, though Lucanus was certain it was because he was the enemy and not because Valimer suspected Lucanus had been fucking his son.

"You said he would be more use alive," Valimer snapped. "Now let's see how much leverage the son of a nobleman has with Honorius's army."

Fear flashed in Gerung's eyes, but he accepted his father's command. Satisfied, Valimer left the tent, ordering that Asbad follow. Asbad obeyed, snarling a few choice insults at Lucanus as he pushed through the tent flaps.

Gerung threw a musty brown tunic in Lucanus's lap. "Put that on."

"What are you going to do?" Lucanus asked.

"I do not know."

Lucanus had just pulled the old tunic over his head when he heard the commotion outside the tent. Women screamed. Children wailed. Men shouted. War cries ended with final breaths. The air was suddenly thick with smoke.

Gerung had his sword in one hand and grabbed the Roman's arm with the other. "I think I know how we can end this."

Outside the tent, they were confronted by the carnage of the attack. Bodies were scattered about. The barbarians were succeeding at keeping most of the Roman soldiers to the edges of the camp, though a few got past to slay any *Vesi* tribe members who had the misfortune of crossing their paths, be they man, woman or child.

The Roman and the young barbarian walked toward the fighting, Lucanus now holding Gerung's sword. Gerung's hands were tied behind his back.

As they approached the combatants, Lucanus shouted out in Latin: "You need not kill them all when capturing one will do!"

One of the Romans in command heard him and demanded to know Lucanus's identity.

"I am Lucanus, son of Trajan Papirius of Perusia. Last night I was taken prisoner by these savages—"

"Savages?" Gerung said indignantly.

"But now, as you see, my fortunes have changed," Lucanus said, waving the sword. The Roman soldiers laughed.

Not laughing, though, was Asbad, now on his horse, his shoulder bleeding profusely. "I should have killed you and spared your horse!" he shouted, struggling to brace an arrow with his one functioning arm.

Lucanus brought the tip of the sword to Gerung's cheek. "Are you sure it will be me who takes your arrow?"

Valimer rode up then, shouting at Asbad to stand down. Directing his attention to Lucanus, he said simply, "Spare my son."

Upon realizing Lucanus had the son of the Gothic chieftain, the Roman soldiers raised their spears.

"Put those down," Lucanus said. "We will not kill this man's son. He will come with me as my prisoner." Looking directly at Gerung, Lucanus said, "He will be more use to me—to *us*— alive."

Gerung bowed his head, barely able to suppress his smile.

A LONG WAY HOME

Richard May

I walked among the Persian dead, stepping carefully. They were smaller on the ground than when facing me, mouths and eyes screaming, spears and swords in hand. I looked for someone I might have known, peering into brown faces becoming browner still in death. When I gazed across the former battlefield, the scene was as if an army had gone to sleep, not died.

"What then, priest? Are you giving blessings to the enemy?"

Aristedes's hand was on my shoulder. Together, we watched the dead, remembering our survival. We had fought back to back yesterday and saved each other's lives several times.

"No blessings," I replied, thinking but not saying that Persians and Ionians are not likely to bless one another. In any case, these dead were nonbelievers, at least in Greek gods; my blessing would do them no good.

Aristedes kept his hand upon my shoulder. "Will you bless me, priest?" I gave him a kiss, which is what he wanted. He reached under my battle tunic and squeezed my ass, as one pats a dog one owns. "Shall we continue walking?" he asked and dropped his hand. I looked at him in surprise. He was not much given to walks or reverie. He waggled his eyebrows comically to make me laugh. "There may be some treasures missed. Ah!" he yelled and bent quickly to one of the small prone figures. "A ring. Gold, I'll wager." He bit it. "Yes, gold. Would you like it?" He always thought I should have presents for my sleeping with him. I hadn't yet convinced him I already had the only present necessary.

"No, you keep it."

He threw an arm around my smaller shoulders. Thracians are huge, also hairy and tattooed, nothing like us more compact, more refined Ionians. In some ways we Greeks of the eastern shore are more like Persians. Our blood has undeniably mixed with theirs during so many decades of defeat. We have been won and lost, won and lost. Now Alexander has come, and we are Greeks again.

Aristedes and I entered our tent. "Let us bathe," I suggested.

"Let us not," he replied, guiding me onto the bed. Aristedes was always ready for sex but especially after battle. He had plunged his sword into so many soldiers and now he wanted to plunge a different weapon into me. He removed my tunic and ran his fingers across my chest.

"You have a beautiful chest, priest." He pinched a nipple and pulled the other, making me gasp. "Lie down," he said, in a voice already hoarse with sex, and followed me onto the bed, pushing my legs back and entering me quickly. While his fat cock stabbed me repeatedly, I listened to his deep grunts and thought of home. His huge, stinking body disgusted me, but he was a friend of our commander. His access to Alexander was the gift I wanted.

I massaged his back and ass as he liked and moaned a little to make him think I liked his fucking. He came quickly with grunts and roars. It was just as well. I could hear someone clearing his throat outside our tent. I tried to stand.

"Now you, beautiful." He pulled me back down, taking my cock in one rough hand and manipulating my chest with another. Before long, I was truly moaning as quietly as I could, writhing beneath him. I spurted into his hand, trying not to shout. "That's better," he said in a self-satisfied coo.

The voice outside cleared itself more loudly. The messenger could tell we were done. He became brave enough to speak.

"My lords, King Alexander requires your presence for council."

"Tell his majesty we will be there immediately," I called to him through our thin canvas walls. I heard his footsteps hurry off. Aristedes and I washed quickly and rushed into cleaner clothes. We checked the state of each other's hair and headed toward the meeting.

Our lord and god incarnate greeted us. "Ah, the Ephesians and Thracians are here at last. Don't tell us why you dallied; we can guess." He teased us while we found our seats, me with the other Ionians and Aristedes among his blue-tinctured Thracians.

Alexander thanked us for his victory and asked how it went with our men, how many killed, how many wounded. The reports were good. We had lost relatively few, and they were already buried in this strange land. I had said words over as many as I could. Soldiers seemed better comforted by a soldier-priest than the temple kind. I had wanted to be the temple kind, but it was my bad luck to be born a prince.

We discussed our next move or, rather, Alexander spoke and we listened.

"The Persians are routed, but they will reassemble. Thousands were killed, but there are tens of thousands more. Reports say they are moving here." Alexander stabbed at a name on the map. "We will confront them again there. Another victory, and Persia will be ours." I liked Alexander. He always said ours, not mine.

I knew my Persian geography. "Sochi," I said aloud.

"Yes, Sochi," Alexander confirmed. I made my face impassive, but he saw something in it still.

"Speak, Ephesus."

"It is a narrow way, my lord."

"It is the closest way." His expression forbade any further discussion. If his Macedonians did not object, why should the rest of us?

We received our individual orders and a fine dinner of lamb stewed in cumin, cilantro and caraway, with rice steamed in saffron and eggplant broiled in basil and pistachios, all served on gold plates taken from some previously conquered town. From north to south and west to east, gluttony decreased and table manners improved. The Macedonians, Illyrians and Thracians crammed meat and bread into their mouths as fast as they could. They were sick of fish. Aristedes joined them in their rush, even though he had eaten better at my table. I tried not to be disgusted by him.

After dinner, we said our good nights and went to see about our men. Neither Ionians nor Attic Greeks would be happy to hear we would be on the march again so soon.

When I came into their campfires, my Ephesians were drinking red Ramian wine and parading silk caftans taken from deserted Persian camps. Their commanders called them to attention and I gave them the news. There were groans and grumblings, but I fired their minds with martial speech and allusions to even greater booty on the road ahead. I know what motivates men.

I sat and drank with them awhile, sure that Aristedes would be doing the same with his Thracians. But at a relatively early hour I got to my unsteady feet and told them all to go to bed. Of course, they laughed good-naturedly at me and ignored my words. I wobbled my way to our tent. How it became a mutual dwelling I remembered clearly. After Ephesus was liberated, Aristedes had appeared and all thoughts of my wife and children had momentarily vanished with the look in his eyes and the touch of his hands. The next morning, when he told me of his connection to Alexander, I began to make my plans. I would be more than a noble nobody in the dust of Alexander's column.

At our tent, when I opened the entrance curtain, he was already there and naked. He was as drunk or drunker than I, but still demanded I undress and lie beside him. Yes, he is a little rough and, yes, uncouth, but I never expected a philosopher. I lay down as he demanded and his thick, hairy arms and thicker, hairier body enveloped me. His cock was hard and urgent. With few preliminaries—barely a kiss—he entered me, ready to fuck. He could come several times a day, sometimes several times in succession.

I played with my chest and jerked my cock, Aristedes holding himself upright above me, watching me writhe. He began to move again inside me, slowly at first—at least for him—then more aggressively. His thick cock sliding in and out of me felt a little less abhorrent. I closed my eyes with simulated delight. Each time I opened them, Aristedes was smiling down at me, his cock pneumatic in my ass.

We came in a cacophony of his groans and my moaning, my seed melding us from two into one. He pulled out of me, gave me a kiss and rolled onto his side, an arm and hand supporting his woolly head.

"Sing for me, priest."

His favorite songs were about love and birds and gentle long-ings. I had learned them all. He needed songs sometimes, when his brain ran on and his heart pounded, especially in the middle of the night when the nightmares came. Then, it was my arms that surrounded him and my body that comforted his.

The next day, we roused ourselves and our men, broke camp and began a new day's march. Aristedes's Thracians marched out of order with us Ephesians near the rear of the column, at my bedmate's request and Alexander's acquiescence. Aristedes had been an exiled prince at Philip's court in Macedonia and learned words and fighting from the same teachers as Alexander. He helped his friend defeat his Thracian uncle.

Scouts said the Persians were not amassing ahead after all; they were behind us. The Greek army turned to meet them at Issus, a town of no importance on a stream barely qualified to be called a river. Aristedes and I grew excited. This would be our chance. Ionians and Thracians were now the head of Alexander's army. We would defeat the Persians and I might kill one in particular. My blood raced and my mind whirled. Darius, where was he?

Aristedes and I drove our men hard into the dust now raised by churning masses, stabbing at every small body wearing pants. Persians fell like rain, a red flow that stained the trampled ground around us and settled the dust.

Aristedes and I stood back to back, although my head came only to his shoulders and his ass nestled above mine. I could feel sweat coursing down my back and didn't know whether it was mine or his. We slashed and cut, hacked and tore at Persians lunging at us from all sides. More than once I had to use a foot to pry my weapon out of a man. My arm was stronger pushing the sword in than pulling it out. Once I caught Aristedes looking over his shoulder at me, laughing at my predicament.

Bodies carpeted the ground around us. When the Persians broke and ran, we chased after them across this carpet, adding more bone and blood to the weave. At some point I stopped chasing after the cowards and looked for Aristedes. He had found a toy and was bringing him to me. The terror in the young man's eyes did not affect me. His fathers and grandfathers had enslaved mine. He would have killed me—or Aristedes—today if he could have.

"Pretty, isn't he?" Aristedes asked, pulling down the boy's trousers. He was unusually handsome in form and face, deeply tanned and dark of eye and hair.

"Yes," I agreed, not sure he seemed wealthy enough to hold for ransom.

Aristedes ripped the Persian's tunic off. "Let us both have him here." He looked eager.

It was something some men did on the battlefield, taking ass as well as gold, but I never had. Aristedes had, I supposed. His passions had certainly risen high; I could see the evidence protruding from his tunic.

"No," I said. "We have work to do. Let us see to our men."

"No!" Aristedes screamed, bringing me to a halt a step away. "I will have this man or he will die!"

I turned and looked into the Persian's eyes. "Let him die then." With those words from me, Aristedes slit the young man's throat and he joined his brothers at our feet. Aristedes stepped across his back to me.

"Let you and I fuck here then," he said defiantly, grabbing my hand and dragging me after him.

"Not here," I told him, but he ignored me, looking for a more private spot. I could see the state he was in and searched with him. I could deny him the Persian, but not myself. There was an outcropping nearby. I led him there and removed my tunic once we were inside the rocks.

"Thank you!" he exclaimed, pulling off his own thin garment.

Being in the open seemed to bring out the lover in him and the animal in me. Aristedes half kneeled, one thick thigh remaining parallel to the ground, and took me into his mouth, pushing me into him with large heavily calloused hands on my ass. He rubbed my body as he sucked, down my legs and up my stomach, across my chest and ass, snorting occasionally when he gagged.

"You are almost hairless, like a boy," he said, taking a breath, then eased me back inside him. His mouth was tight and wet, like my wife's sweet pleasure hole. Though it felt good, I am not an exhibitionist so I hurried him to his feet and took his cock into my mouth, which I knew he wanted. I sucked diligently until his breath was short and quick. He yanked me up then and turned my back to him. I leaned my arms against a boulder while he forced his cock inside me. It seemed larger out of doors. I felt filled, forgetting where I ended and he began. He reached under me for my nipples and twisted, pinched and yanked them while he fucked, his groin pounding hurriedly against my ass, his balls slapping me with each thrust. I tried not to enjoy it, concentrating instead on the battlefield below. The Persian dead spread from our rocks to the river and beyond.

"Make him come," a voice yelled behind and above us. I couldn't tell whether it was Attic or Ionian. I tried to pull away, but Aristedes would not be stopped. He was like a mad bull: having mounted his cow, he was locked in place. One hand took my cock and jerked it rapidly in time to his own rocking motion inside my ass. Like a cow I almost mooed with pleasure and, on hearing sounds from me, he pumped and pulled harder until I came, shouting, whitish globs thick in his hand. With a bellow, he shot his own seed into my ass. The man watching applauded.

"Well done, Thrace and Ephesus. Well done. Now, get dressed. We have a world to win."

"Alexander," Aristedes smirked, not at all ashamed.

"Give me my tunic," I muttered to him, my face red with embarrassment. I avoided looking up until I was dressed. When I looked, there was no one to see.

The Persians ran so quickly from Issus and defeat that they left most of their belongings. I urged that we follow up the rout and make all Persia Greek, but Alexander ignored my advice. We went on to Tyre, Syria and Gaza, fighting our way south rather than east. Alexander was welcomed in Egypt. The battles brought victories and welcome riches. We sojourned at Memphis. All thought of Persia and the East seemed to have vanished from Alexander's head.

One night at yet another banquet, I felt divorced from all

and everyone around me. I thought of Ephesus and of defeating Darius. I drank my wine meditatively.

"Ephesus!"

Alexander was bringing me to attention. He motioned me into his private chambers. I don't think Aristedes noticed. He was too drunk and too busy with his boy. I remembered the rocks above Issus and wondered if Alexander wanted to take a turn with me while my Thracian was distracted. This might be good. However, Hephaestion was already there. I wondered how else to use this opportunity.

"You are thinking, Prince Lysimachus. This is an odd time for thoughts." Alexander indicated the party with a leer over his shoulder.

"I *am* thinking, my lord."

"Tell me."

"Darius, sire. And Persia."

"You want both dead."

I nodded.

"You will get your wish. We turn north in two days. Until then, enjoy yourself." Hephaestion took his hand, while I left them to themselves.

In two days we marched toward Mesopotamia. We crossed the Tigris and Euphrates without opposition. Darius had decided to meet us at Gaugamela, our informers told us. At last, we would destroy the Persian Empire and throne.

At our new camp, on the evening of our arrival, I supervised our tent's reconstruction. Aristedes stood by, joking with other idle men. I had given up asking him to help. Alexander approached and all of us came to attention.

"Come with me, Ephesus," he commanded. Aristedes also stepped forward. "No, my friend. I need someone who speaks Persian. Besides," he chuckled, "you are so gigantic the enemy would see you even in the dark. Your lover and I are both small. Come, Lysimachus." I followed, without a look back. Aristedes had been my hope of reaching Alexander. That hope had been realized.

We rode with hoofs bound with cloth, then walked the last bit to an overhang above the fires of the massive camp. Before we could comment on the panorama below us, Alexander put his finger to his lips. We heard the sentries' horses and hid among the rocks, springing on the riders as they came noisily along. I shouted to them in Persian as they struggled. They all froze at their own language.

I introduced them to Alexander and urged them to speak the truth. It did not take much urging. Within moments, they had told us numbers of men and the location of hidden armaments and traps. Within more moments, they were all dead, killed at Alexander's order. We walked and rode back to our camp of Greeks.

"You did well, Lysimachus," Alexander said once we had dismounted. "You have earned a favor. What is it?" I merely smiled. He laughed at me. "You Ionians! Too subtle for us northern Greeks." Then he laughed again. "Of course, maybe not too subtle for Thracians." He gave me a wink outside his tent, and I walked back to mine.

Aristedes rushed outside as soon as he heard my footsteps. "You're back! I was afraid…" With that he pulled me into our tent and pushed me onto the bed, holding me for a long time without words. His eyes startled me; I could see his soul. I gently urged him back.

"Lie down," I whispered and began to massage his feet, his calves and thighs. When I reached his cock, I stroked it as gently as I had stroked his legs.

"You know what I like, beloved."

I winced at the word. We had never spoken of love. I wasn't sure I was capable of such a lie. Instead of answering, I slid my mouth over his engorged cock, taking it entirely. Aristedes drew a sharp intake of breath.

"You are so good at this, Lysimachus. So good."

His cock filled my mouth to choking and my jaw to breaking. I slid back up the shaft before I gagged, then down again slowly. I was his opposite in lovemaking; I knew how to elongate pleasure. He tried to roll on top of me, but I held him still, my body on his legs, my hands working up his hairy forearms to his massive biceps and bulging chest. There I squeezed the mounds and had him moaning like a woman. Perhaps tonight he would let me fuck him.

But it was not to be. With a steady rise and roll, he maneuvered me beneath him on the bed and then it was short work before my legs were on his shoulders and his cock up my ass, insistent and rapid. I played with my chest and jerked my cock and rolled my head back and forth. Aristedes liked the effect.

"Come first, my beauty," he whispered into my ear before he bit. I followed his instruction and jerked and pinched myself until my back was arching, holding his weight above me. It was then, in a rush, that he came, seconds after I spurted my aromatic seed between us. "Oh, oh, oh!" he yelled, as if he were wounded.

He came in aftershocks for several seconds, his mouth on mine, hands holding my head in place. "That was the best, beloved," he said, giving me a final kiss before he withdrew his cock. For the first time, I felt a strange emptiness and wished him back inside me, but he enclosed me in his arms and fell asleep so I repressed that unwelcome feeling and let him slumber. We would both need our rest for Gaugamela.

When the battle came, we were more than ready, Greeks and mercenaries alike. Days had been spent in training and planning, nights in drinking and bravado. At last, Alexander told of his intention to strike, in council and to the men. I was sure I would not sleep that night, but Aristedes was more attentive to my needs in bed than usual and afterward we both drifted off and slept well. I trusted in our sentries' honor and in Darius's cowardice.

The next morning, we took our places again near the rear of

the army, waiting for the dust cloud to rise ahead. There would be no Issus for us here—the last would not be first—but I knew there *would* be plenty of Persians for all Greeks to slaughter. Darius though would fall to other men, if he did not run again.

The dust cloud rose and the shouting with it. We marched slowly forward and then ran when an opening appeared. Ephesians and Thracians moved into it as a wedge, with Aristedes and myself at the point, parting men as we passed. I began to believe we might be essential and to hope again that I might kill Darius with my own hands.

We cut down Persians left and right, thrusting with pikes, slashing with swords, blood spurting onto our hair and clothes, limbs detaching from our enemies, helmets falling faster than heads. On and on we pushed, farther and farther into them, ignoring their cries, aiming for Darius. I could see him, standing on his gilded chariot, gazing frantically in all directions.

"Stop, Lysimachus!" Aristedes yelled into my ear. "We are surrounded!"

We did seem to be the only Greeks among the Persians. I did not want my men enveloped, so I instructed a runner to reconnoiter our position vis-à-vis the front. He returned, astounded.

"Alexander is behind us!"

"Behind us?" It was hard to hear through the cries of battle and of dying.

"Yes, Prince Lysimachus. Behind us. He is urging us forward."

"Then forward it is!" I said to him and returned to butchering. "Let Alexander follow *us*," I said more softly, which was good because he was suddenly there beside me.

"Well done, priest! Where is Darius? Ah, there. Here man, lend me your spear." A stunned Ephesian yeoman handed his weapon over to our great king and god.

I watched Darius while Alexander hefted the unfamiliar spear onto his shoulder. I damned such bad luck after good to have worked my way through the masses to the coward king, and yet not be able to take the chance to kill him. I tried once.

"Here, my lord. I will handle it for you. These Ionian spears are a little different."

"I think I have it, Lysimachus. Stand clear."

I reluctantly stepped aside and watched as he sent the shaft toward Darius's shriveled heart. I listened, too. Something about the song the missile sang in its travel through the air was off. It would not strike its mark.

It did not, passing inches from Darius's wild-eyed face, close enough to send him on his heels again. He jumped from his chariot onto a convenient horse and disappeared into the mob.

"May you split!" Alexander cursed. I thought to myself it was a little late for that. He turned to me, smiling. "We almost did it though, didn't we?" He was probably happiest at moments such as these, with the canceling shouts of men and clamor of swords.

We attended again to killing every Persian within reach. Alexander and his guards drifted left and we drifted right. As word of Darius's personal retreat spread, his men followed and Aristedes and I stopped to talk. "Let other men take the hunt," he said, his hands on my shoulders, holding me in place. "You should have thrown that spear," he said next.

"Yes," I agreed. "I should have."

He busied himself with accepting presents from the dead while I wondered what it would take to kill Darius. My answer came the next day. Alexander confirmed the rumor at our council: Darius had been assassinated by one of his own generals. I asked to see Alexander alone that night and he agreed.

I bathed carefully and put on my best clothing. My servant curled my hair in the Ionian way. I went to Alexander while Aristedes was busy with his men.

"Welcome, Prince Lysimachus. Would you have some wine?" He filled a flagon for me and drank from his. I bent my head back with drinking and then, thus fortified, began to ask my boon.

"My lord, I have stayed with you faithfully—"

"And now you want to return to Ephesus."

"Yes," I stammered out. "How did you know?"

"Why else would you come alone to me at night in your royal robes and scented body?" He patted the cushions beside him. "Sit here."

When I had settled, he asked the one question I thought he might.

"What of Aristedes?"

I sat up as erectly as I could and gave the demigod look for look. "He is King of Thrace. I will be King of Ephesus. What future can we have together with such responsibilities, at such a distance?"

"You have a cold heart, Lysimachus, but a warm body," Alexander said, reaching inside my garment. He flicked my left nipple casually back and forth, watching my body react. I closed my eyes and licked my lips for him, thrusting out my chest to meet his touch. "There will still be a cost," he said. "I have wanted you from Issus on. Are you prepared to pay?"

I stood and removed my clothing as if my actions had been broken into parts. I presented myself to him, while he looked at me appraisingly. "Yes," he said. "It is how I remember." And then he pulled me down to him again.

While he caressed my cheek and kissed my lips, I thought of Hephaestion. While he pinched and soothed my nipples, I thought of Aristedes, but when he raised my legs and placed them on his shoulders, I thought of home.

After an oddly uninterrupted hour, my lord and new master smiled that he was through and handed me a prepared scroll. Perhaps he *was* a god to have such clairvoyance. I reattached my clothing, straightened my hair and took the signed paper with me. I did not look back.

"Why do you stay with him?" I asked that night in bed with Aristedes.

He fumbled with my body, trying to stop me from thinking and talking. I pushed him away. He tried again. I jumped up and sat on the stool, watching him. He settled back onto our bed, supporting his huge head with thick furry arms decorated with permanent blue images.

"He is Alexander. He commands; we follow."

"You know he wants to go on. Persia is not enough for him."

Aristedes remained quiet. I hesitated, wondering whether I could tell him. I decided I had to, if not now then soon, very soon.

"I am turning back."

He sat up quickly. "He won't let you."

"He has already agreed."

"No! How?"

I looked at him, and he saw the reason. He was on me in an instant.

"You whore! You sold yourself!"

"I want to go home. My goal was to defeat Persia and keep Ephesus and the rest of Ionia Greek. That is done."

"But what about me?" he bellowed. "Am I nothing to you?"

"We are royal princes. Our lives are not our own."

"They are *here*," he reasoned. "We are together here."

"Eventually, we will be killed or you will return to Thrace."

"Perhaps not." He held me close, almost suffocating me. "Don't leave me, Lysimachus. I love you."

Neither of us had said those words before. Hearing them, I felt some regret. I let him guide me back to our bed. I allowed him to kiss my lips and face, chin and neck. I felt his hands on my chest and his fingers manipulate my nipples. I opened my mouth, and his tongue entered. His hands reached between my legs. I raised them for him, and two fingers eased inside my asshole, caressing the inside of me. When his cock slid in after the fingers had prepared the way, I arched my head back, baring my neck for him as he bit and licked. His groin battered against me, pounding harder and deeper, pushing me down until my legs were against the bed, locked in place by his blue arms. I heard myself moan, "I love you, too," as his cock made mine burst across my stomach and his erupted inside me.

He made love to me most of that night. Finally, he slept, but I did not. I rose at daylight, dressed quietly and went to my men, letting Aristedes sleep. I took nothing but a chain he sometimes wore around his neck.

My men were eager to return home, to live in peace with the wealth they had earned and stolen. They packed quickly.

We started walking through the camp back toward Ephesus. I would return to my wife and children. I would rule Ephesus after my father's death. I would be Alexander's ally, satrap or whatever he might require or want from me. I would forget Aristedes, or at least try. I removed his necklace and made to throw it down to the dirt, but my true voice stopped me.

No! Don't! it said inside me, and for once in my life I listened.

I returned my remembrance of Alexander's Persian war to my neck and commanded my men to travel north and west. We were a long way from home and had begun our return. We had best keep going. Perhaps if Aristedes survived... I pushed the thought from my head.

"Forward," I told my commanders. "Forward!" they yelled to their men. *Forward*, I thought, thinking more of who and what was behind me in a canvas tent on the edge of Asia. I said a prayer and began walking.

THE BOY HE LEFT BEHIND

Riley Shepherd

"Ow! Go slow!"

But Josie didn't go no slower. He just kept pounding, face screwed up and red, eyes closed up tight.

"Feels good, Zeke. Nice 'n' tight. Not like no cow."

I was bent over against a fence post by the creek, pants down, Josie ramming up into me, like to split me open. He went deep and I screamed.

"Hush! Someone'll hear!"

"It hurts!"

"You wanted it."

Yeah. I'd waited weeks for Josie to give in, to put his cock in my ass, but as he set to fucking me harder, it was the worst pain I'd ever felt—worse'n a hundred hickory switches.

Still, guess my cock's got a mind of its own. Josie started to throb, filling me with seed, and I shot everywhere: into the creek, on my pants, everywhere.

When he pulled out, I took off my pants to wash them in the creek. Couldn't leave no signs for Ma to see. She'd whip me raw if she knew I'd been getting fucked by a boy, that I'd been sucking his cock every day for a month now. Slipped off my shirt, too. Figured we could swim. But when I turned around, Josie was already dressed.

"Aw, can't I see ya naked?"

"Hell no! Oughtta stay away from you, ya dang fairy." He was suddenly angry. "Ain't doin' this again. People's already sayin' yer queer. I don't want 'em sayin' it about me."

"Don't care what anyone says, Josie." I took a deep breath. "I love you."

His jaw dropped. He stepped toward me. I thought he was finally gonna kiss me, like I dreamed about; instead, he swung at me.

Josie's fist caught my jaw and I fell on my bare ass into the creek, tasting blood.

Josie pulled out his knife, a Cherokee knife with a bone handle and a gray iron blade. His dad gave it to him, and he was real proud of it. He waved it in my face. "Don't you never say that again, y'hear? It's unnatural! Yer sick, Ezekiel. Tetched. You've led me to sin against God. Glad I'm gettin' away from you."

I swallowed. "You're really gonna leave?"

He slashed the air with the knife, like he was gutting an imaginary bear. "Yep. Cornwallis is closer every day. He'll burn our houses to the ground, kill our families. I ain't lettin' that happen. I'm joinin' the militia." He pointed the knife at me. "But you, you're a fairy coward, ain't ya?"

"You know I can't leave Ma."

"Yer pa upped and died 'cause he couldn't stand the sight of your fairy ass." He gave a harsh laugh. "Go ahead. Let the British take whatever they want. You'd probably like them British boys' fancy red coats. Drop yer pants and bend right over for 'em."

"I only do that for you, Josie, 'cause—"

THE BOY HE LEFT BEHIND

"Not another word, fairy!" He spat on me. The boy I loved and gave myself to, spat on me and left me sitting in the cold water to cry. It was August, hot, but I shivered. Shivered in the bright summer sun.

"He had you."

I looked up, startled at the voice. It weren't daylight; it was dark. And it weren't August, but October. This was the Mountain Witch's cabin. I'd come for answers, and she'd given me some awful drink, made me see things—memories.

The old woman touched the seat of my pants with knuckles so gnarled they looked like an old shoe chewed by a dog. "He had you here."

My asshole began to throb, like Josie were still inside it. That was weeks ago.

"There was pain," she said.

"Awful pain."

"Sometimes love is pain. Sometimes pain is just...pain."

Something warm and wet touched my chest. The witch painted me with blood.

"What—?"

"Blood seeks blood," she said. "Blood tells."

I didn't ask where she got the blood, just: "Tells what?"

"The fate of him made your blood hot. Josiah is dead."

She said it just like that. Like it weren't nothing. Like you'd say, *it's raining*.

My throat closed up. I just managed, "No."

"Dead. A month gone."

"Liar! Knowed you was a fraud!" I couldn't believe it. Josie dead? Just because this old crone said so?

"He weren't meant for you. Didn't love you."

"Huh? Who are you to say—?"

"There's another, waiting. Meant to be yours and you his. A boy from far away."

I started to say I didn't know no such boy.

"Close your eyes."

"No," I said.

She rapped her gnarled walking stick against the floorboards with a snap like a rifle shot.

It spooked me. I minded.

"Keep 'em shut. Look at the fire. What do you see?"

Seemed silly, looking with my eyes closed. But there was this glow t'other side of my eyelids. "There's...orange light."

"Look into it."

A shadow appeared, the shadow of a young man. He stepped forward, all bathed in fire. The orange cooled-like, to blue, shimmered like water. The boy weren't no shadow anymore. He was lit, like by the sun sparkling on the creek, like he was underwater. He was naked, perfect, his hair also like the sun, eyes like new spring leaves.

I wanted him. Wanted to touch him, feel his skin, kiss him. He smiled at me and then washed away.

I opened my eyes.

"How—?"

"He's waiting," said the Witch.

"But Josie—!"

"Love is pain." She pointed to the door. "Now git. Leave me."

I walked to the creek, where Josie and I had swam and played and fucked. Josie was dead. I'd guessed it before she even said it. He couldn't write much, but I knew he'd have wrote something by now if he were alive. Least to his ma and pa. He'd not.

All because he'd went to war. *"I'uz born to be a warrior."* He'd say it while I sucked his dick and then he'd crow like an Indian brave and blow his seed down my throat.

I didn't want to be no warrior. Just wanted to fuck some ass or get fucked, even if it hurt. When I dreamt of being with another boy, him riding me, dick in my ass, it never hurt. Not in my dreams.

It hurt with Josie, but not half as much as it hurt him calling me "fairy."

I was of age to marry, but Pa died before he could tell me what husbands and wives done together. I learned by watching animals: cows and horses. They fucked in front of me. Didn't have secrets, not like people.

Cows is ugly, though. Their big, saggy teats turned my stomach. Girls was scarce in these hills. Only woman I'd seen naked was Ma. She had big, saggy teats, too. Didn't ever learn to get horny for no girls. But I seen myself naked, and other boys, too. I liked our bodies. Smooth and sleek. No saggy bits, 'cept the dick. And that stopped sagging if you treated it right. If I'uz going to fuck, I wanted to fuck someone who looked like that.

But my someone was gone.

I set with my feet in the creek and cried. Miserable as I was, the water felt good. I stripped and jumped in.

Behind me came a splash; someone was jumping in with me. I tried to turn, but an arm hooked my neck, locked my head in place. Something cold scraped my throat, sharp like a knife.

"Don't move," said a voice, all weak and raspy.

But I did move. I twisted and saw that the blade against my neck was strapped to a rifle. *A bayonet.*

He tightened his grip like to strangle me, but he didn't have the strength. I got my hand where it could protect my throat from the blade. Better cut fingers than a cut throat.

I used to wrestle Josie. Never won, but got lots of practice. I elbowed this feller hard, then threw him off balance and into the creek. Then I stood ready to fight, but realized the poor bastard was passing out.

Well, I couldn't let him bash out his brains on the rocks. I caught him and stood him up. He was smeared with mud, all blackish brown, but there were patches of red in his coat. *A British soldier.*

He was dead weight in my arms. I eased him down and

slapped his face to rouse him. "You're half-killed! When'd you eat last?"

He tried to swallow, winced, shook his head.

"You're in no shape to fight. What got into you?"

"K-kill you...before...kill me." His voice was weak. I had to lean close.

"I wouldn't kill anyone, even a redcoat. Hell, I cain't even let you starve. Let's get you washed, hide that coat, and I'll take you home and feed you."

I peeled off his clothes. They were caked with mud, and he was limp like a rag doll. He was no bigger'n me and bony. What was he doing here with no British regiment nearby?

I helped him into the water, almost forgetting we were both naked. He was so dirty you couldn't tell, 'cept for white spots where his clothes had been. The dirt ran off in streaks. The water got cloudy with mud. Then I looked down and saw his reflection.

My heart jumped. *It was him.* The boy from the Witch's vision.

"Where'd you come from?"

"Bath, England. I was with Lord Cornwallis. I was...separated." Them bright-green eyes were suddenly guilty looking.

"You run, didn't you?"

He nodded. "After the first battle...all those men killed...the blood. I just...started walking."

A deserter. Tories, those men still loyal to the crown, would shoot him if they found him alive. Patriots'd shoot me for helping him. He was my enemy. But, stripped of his uniform, naked flesh under my hands, he didn't seem like no enemy.

I knelt to wash his legs, his manhood in my face. It weren't near as small as he was; it was standing up to greet me.

His face was red. Was he...like me?

"Even *that's* covered in dirt," I said. I took a deep breath and set to washing him there. He jumped at the cold water, but got harder when I touched him. I rubbed off dirt, gentle-like. I reckon I rubbed a little longer than I needed to. He moaned, but he didn't stop me.

"If you don't wash careful here, it gets sore." I worked his foreskin back and forth, running my finger over the head, teasing. He shivered with excitement. I felt brave enough to try more.

"Looks clean, but my friend Josie showed me how to make sure."

I took him into my mouth, like I done for Josie all those times. I ran my tongue over his cock and sucked at it, like a calf at a teat. I was afraid he'd shove me away, but he took hold of my shoulders and pushed forward, pumping into my mouth. I couldn't swallow all of him, but he was easier on me than Josie ever was. Didn't last long, neither. I tasted him, hot and salty, on my tongue.

"Reckon you're clean now."

For the first time, he smiled. It was a good smile. He had all his teeth and they was mostly straight.

"Let's get you fed." I got us dressed and walked him home, an arm around his shoulders.

Ma didn't take to me bringin' no stranger home, but she softened when she heard Duncan was a soldier, wounded, left for dead. Duncan Forsyth was his name. I only knew because Ma asked. Ain't it funny? Here was a boy just spunked in my mouth, and I hadn't asked his name.

We bedded down in the loft. Ma don't sleep there, can't climb the ladder. Duncan didn't manage too well, neither. I had to help him up. It weren't just hunger or exhaustion; something had shaken him bad, hurt his soul.

"Sorry I don't got an extra nightshirt," I said as we undressed.

He shrugged. "At school we often slept without clothes."

"We'll blow out the candle. It won't matter none." I pulled

off my pants and left myself naked. "T'aint fair, me havin' a nightshirt and you not."

Duncan gave the tiniest smile, then took off his own clothes. In the candle glow, he looked like an angel, lit with heavenly light. I studied the white smoothness of his chest, like an ivory sculpture. Tiny pink nipples, smaller'n mine. Not much muscle. Reckon he was a city boy. The hair on his cock was reddish gold and caught the candle's flicker.

I wanted him. Not like I wanted Josie. I wanted to *hold* Duncan, to protect him. I felt like I was the strong one now, where before I'd always been the weak.

After three days, Duncan was strong enough to make it up the ladder hisself, and he started helping with chores. We didn't fool around. I figured he was too weak. I'd play with myself at night, Duncan, warm and naked, asleep with his back to me.

The fourth night, we lay awake, talking. All of a sudden, Duncan says, "It was kind of you to take me in. You shouldn't feel obligated to a coward."

"Ain't cowardly, not wanting to watch people die. Wish Josie had run away."

"Josie?"

"My friend. He went to war. He's dead."

"I'm sorry."

"Yeah."

"Was it Josie who taught you...what we did the other day?"

"Yeah. We done a lot together, things people say are wrong."

"It...didn't feel wrong."

For a minute, we were quiet, and I swear we each knew what the other was thinking.

I reached for him in the pitch black, put my mouth to his. He was surprised at first, but he opened his lips a little and just sort of melted them into mine. Our teeth scraped, which made us laugh. But when his tongue accidentally caught mine, I thought

I'd done died and gone to Heaven.

Josie never let me kiss him.

Duncan's cock was hard against me. I reached down and stroked it. It jumped under my hand. He was close already.

He grabbed my hand and gasped, "I...I want—"

"I know," I said. "I want it, too. I want it bad."

I flipped onto my stomach and arched my back. I knew it would hurt, but I still wanted it. Something tickled me. Something was going into my hole, warm and wet.

"What ya doing?"

"I'm sorry, I thought you wanted—"

"Oh, I want you to fuck me all right. Just, well, no one ever stuck his fingers in my hole."

"How do you loosen up? Doesn't it hurt?"

"Yeah...a lot."

He leaned in, kissed me. "It needn't."

He worked his finger in slow. I started to buck and beg for more. Then he done two fingers. It stung, but I got used to it, pushed back, driving them into me as deep as they would go. Not enough.

My body asked for more all on its own. Right quick I felt his big cockhead stretch my hole. I gritted my teeth, expecting pain, but he slipped inside me. It didn't hardly hurt.

Duncan held still, rubbing my back while I got comfortable. "Is this all right?" he asked.

I grunted, not in pain, but just because there was so much *feeling*.

"Please...*fuck me!*"

And he done fucked me, hard and fast as Josie ever did. Harder. But still no pain. He was hot and sweaty against me, his breath warm in my ear and blowing across my face.

He yelped and I felt warmth inside me. It set me over the edge. I spewed and covered the blankets with more than I'd ever shot before.

I rolled to my side, Duncan spooning against me.

"Where'd you learn that?" I asked, "using your fingers 'n' all?"

"School. Boys bugger each other at school."

"Never been," I allowed. I stroked his cheek. "Did you like... that?"

He squeezed me tight. "*So* much. And I love *this*. Just holding you. I feel warm and—just *safe*. I haven't felt safe since England."

"You're safe. No one can hurt you."

He snuggled in and kissed me. "You are my savior, Ezekiel."

We fell asleep all curled up together, me and Duncan.

Me and the boy I was fated to find.

I woke to nature's call, Duncan still wrapped around me. I gently pried him loose, rolling out from under the blankets, naked, morning's chill a shock after spending the night warmed by his body.

"Ow!" I'd rolled onto something hard and cold. It dug into the small of my back. I reached under and pulled it out into daylight.

Duncan grinned. "Sorry. I forgot that was in my pocket."

He forgot.

But I couldn't forget. Never. Not the feel of it in my hand, the glint of it in the light. Disbelieving, I held it afore me. At first I closed my eyes, didn't want to see. Didn't want to know what it *had* to mean.

"What's wrong?" asked Duncan.

I had to open my eyes, let them see what my fingers already told me. I was holding a knife.

Josie's knife.

"Where'd you get this?" My throat was almost too closed up to talk.

"Charlotte. The battlefield."

"It's Josie's."

Duncan went pale. "I...I didn't know, I..."

I forced myself to say the awful thing it had to mean. "You... you killed him, didn't you?"

I crawled over, grabbed his face, made him look at me. "*Didn't you?*"

He was mute. Helpless. Like an animal that knows it's about to be eaten alive.

I punched him in the chest. "You killed him!"

He coughed. "I...I didn't mean to."

I pressed the knife against him. "I should cut your fucking throat!"

Eyes wide, he raised his chin, showing his throat.

"Do it," he sobbed. "Please."

So help me, I thought about it. About what it would feel like to dig the point in, tear his flesh, open his veins.

He whispered, "Please."

But I couldn't. I flung the knife into the eaves and then I punched him, over and over. Tears came to my eyes. I couldn't see what I was doing.

"Land sakes, what's going on up there?"

I'd forgot Ma was downstairs, forgot she was alive at all. I didn't answer. I put on pants and near fell down the ladder. I ran out into the cold of morning, cutting my bare feet on stones, not caring. I ran deep into the woods, away from the house, away from Ma, away from the boy.

The boy I was fated to find.

"Well? What d'ye want now?"

I didn't answer the Witch. Couldn't. Just stood at her door, the knife in my hands like some kinda offering.

She snatched it. Looked it over. "This was Josie's."

"Yes."

"How'd you get it?"

"From the boy. The boy you showed me...before."

"The boy you gave yourself to last night."

I didn't even stop to wonder how she knew. I just nodded. "He killed Josie."

"I know it. Why did you come here?"

"'Cause nothing makes sense, that's why. How could someone like Duncan be a killer? And where is Duncan? I left him when I found the knife. He was gone when I came home."

"You want to kill him yourself?" she asked.

"Dunno what I want. Last night, I thought I'uz..." I couldn't say the words out loud.

"In love?"

My face burned. "That's a sin."

The Witch spat in the dust. "Ain't no sin to love, boy. Ain't never."

"It's surely a sin to love him who killed someone *you loved*."

She gave a wet sigh. "Men...boys...die in war. Do they deserve it? What if Josie killed Duncan? Would that make Josie evil? Josie went to war to kill British."

"They's...our enemies."

"Ye send young men into battle. Ye tell them it's right to kill each other. Then ye hate them for doing what they're told?" She cocked her head at me. "D'ye know *how* Josie died?"

"No."

She got up, crossed the room, went to the fire. She lifted a pot from the coals and poured liquid from it into a cup. She'd done the same thing last time.

"Drink it."

I shook my head. "I don't want to. It'll give me visions again, and I don't wanna see."

She shoved the cup in my face. "Ain't about what ye *want* to see. It's about what ye *have* to see. What ye have to *know*."

* * *

It was daylight, bright, warm. But the air was full of smoke and screams. Men were all around, some red-coated, some not. Patriots, Englishmen, Tories.

Shots sounded. Horses' hooves thundered. I spun around to avoid being trampled, but there weren't no danger; I wasn't really there. Within arm's reach crouched a figure in bright red, trembling. A scream behind us startled him. He turned.

Duncan.

His coat was clean, new. This was his first battle. He backpedaled, trying to get away from the screaming. I turned and someone passed right through me. Didn't hurt. Felt like *nothing.*

It was Josie, alive. My heart skipped a beat. But I remembered this was just a vision.

This was Josie's death.

Josie shrieked again as he charged Duncan. His knife was gripped tight in his hand, pointed at Duncan's heart.

Duncan was so afraid he couldn't move. Another few seconds and Josie's blade would be in his chest. But it didn't happen that way. Duncan's trembling hands managed to raise his rifle. It caught Josie's breastbone and stopped him running. Josie slashed out with that knife like a madman. Once he caught Duncan on the side of his neck. Duncan winced with pain, closed his eyes...

That's when he fired.

The shot blew Josie backward. He tripped and, before he fell, he looked down at the bloody hole in his chest, surprised. He hadn't thought he could actually die.

I tried to scream, like in a bad dream, when you try to holler and nothing comes out. I ran forward to hold Josie, but I couldn't touch him. I wasn't really there. I could only look into Josie's eyes as they started to cloud over. He gave a little shake and he was gone.

Duncan cried out as though *he* were the one wounded. He knelt right where I was, shook Josie's shoulders and begged him not to be dead. Duncan's eyes were wild, senseless. His tears fell over Josie, over his first kill in his first battle.

Duncan pressed Josie's knife in that dead hand, tried to close the fingers 'round it, but a bullet whizzed by his ear. Still clutching the knife, he dropped, scrambling backward, toward the woods. Then he got up and ran, away from the battle, away from the boy he'd killed.

The boy I loved.

I cried over Josie, unable to touch him.

I was still crying when the Witch stroked my hair, bringing me back.

"He didn't mean to do it," I said. "Duncan didn't mean to kill anyone. He was just afraid." I wiped my face on my sleeve. It was time to stop crying and do something useful.

"Can you tell me where he's gone?" I asked.

"Back to his regiment. To die like he thinks he deserves. Like he thinks you want him to."

"It wasn't his fault," I whispered.

"He's halfway to King's Mountain. There'll be a battle there. Hundred or more Tories will die."

"Will Duncan die?"

"It's up to you, Ezekiel. Will you ride to King's Mountain?"

Me? Ride into battle?

"I don't know nothing about fighting."

The Witch held up the knife. "This can protect ye."

"Didn't help Josie none."

"It's got the power of a boy's first love in it." She touched it to my neck, just below my ear. "It's tasted blood. Duncan's blood still stains the blade."

She showed me the knife's edge with its dark, brownish stain.

"It joins Duncan and Josiah by blood. You love both. Were it to taste your blood, that would be a powerful enchantment. Love, regret, hope...all inside."

THE BOY HE LEFT BEHIND

She wanted to cut me, to mix our blood.

"Do it," I said.

She cut quick. At first it stung, then it was like my neck was on fire. I screamed and slapped my hand over the wound. Only there weren't no wound. Weren't no blood, neither.

The Witch held out the knife to me in both her hands. "Enchanted by blood, by love for the living and for the dead. It'll protect you. Go, Ezekiel. Ride. Follow the knife. Follow your love."

I'd never been outside the holler where I was born. Didn't exactly know where King's Mountain was, though I knew it wasn't far. Still, somehow, the route was in my head. Maybe it was just whatever the Witch done to that knife or maybe it was Josie's spirit guiding me, but anytime I started to take a wrong turn on the way, a voice in my head set me right.

After a day or so, I spotted the Overmountain men, the Patriot militia headed for King's Mountain. They were set to surprise the enemy who'd been threatening the Carolinas. They didn't wear uniforms. Duncan had said the Tories didn't neither. The Patriots were rough-looking, proud, hardworking men, out to defend their homes and families.

They were pinning bits of white paper to their hats, so they'd know who was Tories and who was Patriots. That struck me funny, riding into battle against people so like yourselves that you needed a marker to know who to kill.

Duncan would be with the Tories, not here. The Witch hadn't been wrong yet. So I'd make my way over the mountain ahead of these men, before they struck. I stood up from my hiding place and ran up the hill.

The bank was wet from rain. It was slick going. I fell a couple times. But I was raised in the hills, knew how to pull myself up using vines and creepers. I was winded when I came into sight of the Tories. They'd camped on the mountainside and were packing up. A man on a big white horse rode among them, blowing on a silver whistle, saying to hurry up, be ready to move out.

Where was Duncan? I had to find him. I came over the rise and into their midst. I walked from man to man, searching. Nobody seemed to notice me. The enemy, after all, was going to attack in force, not send one lone farmboy.

I was near the ruins of a campfire when I heard the man on the horse call out, "Here, Forsyth, put this sprig of pine bough into your hat. We might shoot you otherwise."

I turned. There was Duncan, dirty and ragged, in borrowed clothes too big for him, but he was my Duncan. Yes, *mine*.

I called out, waving, but Duncan didn't look my way. He couldn't hear me from that distance, it seemed. But he had to, if I was going to save him.

I clutched the knife handle and called out again. This time Duncan looked up, startled.

Someone big and strong grabbed me. Before I knew it, I was on the ground and a Tory soldier stood over me, a sneer on his face. I guess he was a bit more suspicious than the rest, for he shouted, "Colonel! Here's a damned spy!"

The Tory whipped round his rifle and drove the bayonet point against my throat.

"Kill him," somebody called out. "Before he calls for help."

The Tory reared to drive the blade into me. In my hand, the knife heated up. Before I could think, it had slashed up and out. The knife struck the Tory in his throat. Warm blood splashed me as he fell.

Men gasped around me. In seconds, they'd be on me. I pulled the knife away and lifted it up in the air, its end smeared with red.

I saw fear in the Tories' eyes, but one man, shouting, raised his rifle and fired before I could think. Either he missed or he'd not loaded the ball. I wasn't shot. I put my hand to my throat, felt the ridge of torn flesh where the bayonet had bit into it.

The Tories came at me, shouting for blood. They circled around, grabbing at me. I spun faster than I ever moved in my life, lashing out with my knife, slicing any flesh that came near. A man screamed as I opened up his wrist to the bone. That only made the rest angrier. I slit one across his belly. As he fell into me, my arm propelled itself up and back, sinking the weapon into the eye of a man behind me. The sound and feel made me want to puke.

Four enemies were down, done in by Josie's knife, like Josie was somehow there, protecting me.

Up the hill suddenly came a noise like a million demons shouting. The man on the horse whistled his troops to ready.

The Tories forgot me as the Patriots spilled over the ridge like a creek flooding. Rifle shots rang out. The charging men with bayonets fell. Mountain men know how to shoot. Still, under the crazed assault of the bayonets, the Patriots started to give ground.

I'd lost sight of Duncan in that mass of men heading down the hill. I reckoned I had made it this far, still alive, so I waded into the battle.

It had to be a half an hour or more before I finally found him. He had his rifle held at ready, but he wasn't firing.

I ran toward him. "You're gonna get shot, ya darn fool!"

Out of the corner of my eye, I saw the glint of sunlight on a blade, a Tory bayonet. I leapt forward at my attacker, caught him with my knife, tore a gash down the whole of his arm.

He fell, shrieking at Duncan. "Kill him, Forsyth!"

Duncan's lip quivered. "I...I can't."

The man tried to lurch at both of us, then pitched his face in the mud. There was a bullet hole clean through his head. Up came a grizzled fellow with a rifle, a piece of dirty white paper shoved into the brim of his hat. Behind him came another Tory, his rifle aimed at our Patriot savior.

My knife shot up, almost on instinct now. It caught that Tory hard in the throat and he fell. The Patriot looked back at me, grinned, then went to free my knife from the gurgling throat of the dying man. He scooped up the rifle the Tory had dropped, too, and handed them both to me.

"You'll kill more with this." His eye caught the sprig of pine in Duncan's cap. "You can practice your aim on that scrawny target."

"No," I said, making my eyes hard as I looked on the face of the fair British boy I loved. "No bullet for him. He's mine."

I raised my knife, threw myself at Duncan and knocked him to the ground. I hoped the Patriot would move on, wishing that Duncan would fight me, to make it look good, but he just went limp. I raised and looked him in the eye.

He was in tears. "Just do it quickly, please."

He still thought I was there to kill him. He wanted me to.

"Shut up," I said. "No one's killing you. I said you're mine and I meant it."

"Step away, boy. I'll get the limey bastard."

The Patriot still watched, his gun trained on Duncan's head. I didn't have no choice but to throw the knife. It was Duncan or the Patriot who'd saved my life. Loyalty meant nothing to me, not up against love. The Patriot died with Josie's blade in his heart.

"How did you find me?" Duncan finally wondered aloud.

I shrugged. "The Witch's enchantment, I s'pose." Though maybe it was something else, something more powerful that led me to him.

A storm of rifle shots nearby reminded me we were still in danger. "Play dead," I said and fell down on him, sheltering him, kissing his neck once, secretly, where Josie's knife had scarred him.

It was like layin' low in a thunderstorm. The battle raged around us. I prayed for us not to be seen or, worse, trampled.

Men fell dead, some so close I could touch them. The man on the white horse rode up high on the hillside, blowing his whistle. The Patriots saw him and fired. A half-dozen bullets riddled him and he dropped from the horse.

Soon after, the Tories ran up a white flag. "It's almost over," I whispered to Duncan. "They're surrendering."

But the shots kept up. The wounded moaned, some calling out for their mamas.

Finally a voice called out, "Don't kill any more!"

The shots stopped. I stayed still and listened to marching feet, heard men begging. Hundreds of Tories were led away as prisoners.

They didn't bother with us on the ground, even if we were moving. One of the Patriot colonels said they needed to clear out fast. Cornwallis and a bigger army might be coming. "Leave the wounded to die."

I must have fallen asleep. I woke to moonlight, Duncan still there, only I was curled up around him now. His face was painted all silver by the moon. He looked like an angel. I hated to wake him, but now was the time to get away. Tomorrow, they'd come for the wounded and they wouldn't let a Patriot and the enemy leave together.

I whispered, "Duncan." His eyes opened. I took his shoulder and set him upright. "Let's go. T'ain't safe here."

He rubbed his eyes. "Why did you come here?"

"To save you."

"But I killed your friend."

"Don't ask me how, but I saw what happened. Josie was going to kill you. In battle, you kill to stay alive. Good reason not to get into battle, I s'pose."

His head hung. "I deserved to die like all these men."

I grabbed his shoulders, shaking him hard. "No. I told you. You're mine, and I'm not letting you die."

He stared, eyes filling with tears. I leaned forward and kissed him, kissed him for a long time. Only stopped when I felt my cock stirring. This weren't the place to start no lovemaking, though.

I jerked my head toward the woods. "Let's go."

"Where are we going?"

"Home."

He almost laughed. "Where's home?"

I kissed him again. "Wherever we're safe together."

GIFTED

A. R. Bell

Nobody knew where he had come from. Some said that one unusually hot night in August, a star had fallen from the sky and landed right by the eastern wall of Putna Citadel. When people rushed to the spot, it was so hot and smoky that no one could get near and the next day Bogdan was presented as the new captain of Moldova's army. Others claimed that he was the illegitimate son of the late Lady Ileana, hidden from the sight of the people until he was fifteen years of age for fear of curses. However, it was the first story that seemed the most plausible, since nothing could go on in the Citadel without the nosy maids finding out and gossiping about it the kitchens.

Bogdan was tall and of a rather dark complexion, with eyes so black and deep that old women felt the need to make the sign of the cross and whisper a little prayer every time they passed him in the square. He'd fought many battles against the invading Turks and came back victorious in most. Radu, the King of Moldova, held him in great esteem and not a day went by without him seeking Bogdan's council. Today was no exception, as they both sat in the tent raised by the Black Sea. It was a cold, windy evening and the water seemed to foresee the bloody battle that was about to unleash itself on its peaceful shore.

"We should not have come here," Bogdan said, gazing upon his lord, who was eating a piece of cold lamb steak. "We should have stayed in Putna and waited for them there."

"They would have pillaged our villages and burned our crops on their way. It's our duty to defend our people, not only our castle."

"Your people…" Bogdan began, but stopped as he saw Radu getting up and coming very close to him.

"Our people. Mine and yours."

The young captain remained silent. Radu was only five years his elder. He had a larger frame and golden hair that hung down upon his shoulders. His countenance was mean enough to freeze any enemy solider in his tracks and his strong arms had slain many of them, to be sure. Moldova was ruled with an iron fist, and all those who wronged against it suffered the cruelest of fates. Bogdan was probably the only one who didn't fear the Moldovian ruler and made a habit of challenging his decisions and second-guessing his actions. Still, aware of the proud nature of the King, he only acted like this in private. Tonight was no exception.

"We are outnumbered, M'lord."

"Bogdan, for the one thousandth time, stop calling me that when we are alone."

"Fine," came the reply, though he well knew he would never stop calling him this. "There will still be a lot more Turks than us," he then added.

"I know. But they do not expect us to be waiting for them here."

"Many of us will perish."

"They will die in glory."

"Maybe I will—"

Bogdan was stopped mid-sentence by the Moldovian King, who had once more got up and violently pushed him.

"You will never, *ever*, say that again. You are my captain and you will not only live but come out of it unscarred. Is that clear?"

"It is not up to you." Bogdan pushed him back. "Not this time."

"Bogdan...I wish for you to live."

"Why? I have been wondering just that for five years now. Why is my life so precious to you? Why did you—?"

"Enough!" Radu's voice thundered. "We need to rest. The enemy will be here at dawn, and may God help us."

"We might have upset Him with our daring. I think we will lose."

"I'll wager you we won't."

"What do you wager?"

The King managed the briefest of grins. "If we come away victorious, I want you shaved."

"And if we lose?"

"If we lose, I'll give you whatever you wish."

"I want *to know*." The words hung there. They both knew their meaning.

"So be it."

The two men were only inches from each other, the royal tent now suffused with a heavy air.

"Good night, M'lord," Bogdan said, literally running out while Radu stood there trying to compose himself. He needed to win this battle, not only for Moldova but for himself.

Back in his own tent, the captain was getting ready for sleep when a young boy came in apologizing for the intrusion but saying he had a message. Bogdan didn't need to ask from whom.

"What is the message?"

"Well..." the boy stammered, "the message is, *It's not about your beard.*"

Bogdan instantly blushed and sent the boy away, giving him a silver coin for his trouble. Sleep did not find him that night, as all he could think of was Radu's indecent message. Had he really meant what he thought? His heart was pounding hard, his cock even harder.

So much blood had been spilled at Adamclisi before noon on that mid-November morning that the angry waves of the stormy sea could not wash it away for days. Hungry sharks came from miles around to feast on the mutilated bodies. The beach was an even more frightful sight.

The Turkish ships had arrived as expected at sunrise and the brave Moldovians were there to give them the greeting of their iron swords. They fought for hours, and over five thousand souls went to the Heavens that day, some to meet Allah, some to be welcomed by Saint Peter. In the end, the Muslims waved their white flags and the ships carrying what was left of their army fled back to Istanbul, while the Christians were left tired and victorious on the shore to tend to their wounded and mourn their dead.

Once the infernal clamor subsided, Radu looked around and met Bogdan's gaze. There was something that made them never lose sight of each other, even in the madness of battle. This time Moldova's ruler strode over and placed his arm around the other man's shoulder. They were quite a sight, the well-built blond man and the slender, dark-haired captain, both covered in thick armor and matted blood.

"We won. I shall see you in my tent. Don't make me wait," Radu said, and though his sentences were short and he tried to seem his determined self, Bogdan could tell that he was flushed. Could the King be as nervous as he was? Bogdan wondered.

He decided not to delay their meeting for too long, so he

made for the royal tent, walking directly to his King. He found him wearing a clean tunic and trousers, his hair combed and tied. He was incredibly handsome, the epitome of power and might.

"Did you receive my message yesterday?" Radu asked without even bidding him welcome.

"You know I did," Bogdan replied, approaching closer and looking straight into the deep-blue eyes of his Sovereign. "Do you want me to do it and then present myself or is it your wish to watch?" he asked, and he was surprised at the effect his own words had on him.

"I will take great pleasure in doing that myself."

"I bet you will."

"Is it wise to keep making bets with me?"

"I lost the ability to be wise around you years ago, as you are well aware."

"Am I now?" Radu suddenly had a sheepish smile on his lips.

Instead of giving him an answer, Bogdan dropped his breeches and stood only in his white tunic.

"Where do you want me?"

At that, the supreme ruler of Moldova lost his composure and grabbed the younger man's head, bringing the captain's mouth to his own in a violent kiss. In all his life, all the battles and the victories, all the traitors he had caught and punished, all the joys and all the sorrows together did not hold the intensity of this one moment. Years of tormented, sleepless nights and feelings of guilt melded into this storming dance of tongues that let Radu know that the man he had craved for all this time wanted him just as badly.

"That did not answer my question," Bogdan eventually said with amazing composure.

"What? How can you? Do you not..." The Sovereign was at a loss for words, a situation he didn't find himself in very often.

"Oh, I do, M'lord, but you have taunted me for so long with

your aloofness that now you will have to play your own game a little longer. Ah, I see you have prepared the basin and razor over here," he said, simply, and kneeled on the soft mattress that was on the floor. "I lost a wager, now I must suffer the consequences."

"It's odd how you have managed to turn your punishment into my torment."

"It serves you well for torturing both of us for the better part of the last five years."

Radu could not believe how this handsome foreigner, who was now on all fours on his mattress in such a servile posture, actually had him, the mighty ruler, eating out of the palm of his hand. But he decided two could dance that dance, and so he took the soap and soaked it for a bit in the basin, then started to lather first his hands, then the soft skin between Bogdan's hairy asscheeks, all the way down, taking the captain's throbbing length into his palm and making it expand even farther. They were both out of breath and neither dared speak for fear that the moment so long waited for would end.

After that, the soap was applied to Bogdan's face. The sharp blade of the razor, which was next lifted up, felt cold on his heated skin. He could hear the scraping as the thick hairs were plowed off him. All of it was most unreal.

Radu was obviously taking his time, running his thumb over each new bald patch. This intimate action held more magic for him than all the stories made up of how this handsome man arrived at his court. Perhaps their encounter had, after all, been from another world. How else could he explain that moment of utter bliss in the middle of the most hellish battle he had ever been a part of? That night, five years prior, he had seen all his trusted captains fall victim to enemy blades. He had all but given up hope when, after the falling of a Turk he had stabbed, there stood this young boy with his dark beautiful eyes. He was armed, but did not motion to attack, and, mesmerized by the depth of his gaze, Radu put down his weapon. On impulse, he grabbed the boy's arm and strode all the way to his tent. Never before had the Moldovian ruler left the field of battle, but at that point, the urge to protect this seemingly magical apparition was stronger than his own patriotism.

The battle had been lost, but Radu was not sad. He found the boy waiting patiently in his tent, right where he had left him, even though he had used no restraints. They traveled back to Putna, and for the following year, he hid this handsome Turk from the world, forbidding everyone to enter his chambers and spending every spare moment teaching him the language of his land.

"You seem distracted from the job at hand," Bogdan said, breaking Radu's train of thought.

"Are you getting cold?"

"Just a little bored. I was hoping for my punishment to be more...*entertaining*."

"And what would entertain you now?" he asked, running his thumb along the freshly shaven skin.

"I think you know very well, M'lord. Since you have so thoroughly plowed the field, you might as well put in the seed."

"How eloquent in Moldovian you have become."

"I had a great instructor, who spent many hours doing nothing else but teach me the proper way to speak it."

"Is there an accusation in that?"

"You know there is."

"As appealing as this view is, Bogdan, I would rather you said it to my face."

The young man turned around and now lay on the mattress with his legs spread and his hands under his head. Radu was in awe of the beautiful circumcised cock that was holding firm, almost in spite of itself.

"I'm accusing you of torturing both of us for far too long. I left my country and my people to be with you. I was yours to do with as you pleased for a whole year, hidden in your chambers, and you not so much as laid a finger on me. Why?"

"You were fifteen!"

"It's been five years since then! Five whole years of torture."

"I just wanted you to be old enough to be certain."

"I am extremely certain," he panted. "Now get undressed and come here!"

"I was under the impression you were mine to do with as I please," Radu said with a smile as he started to undress.

"That was five years ago."

"Still, you lost the wager, so now you shall do as I say. At least this time."

Bogdan growled in frustration.

"What more do you want from me?"

"Everything!" Moldova's ruler barked before collapsing on the mattress next to his captain, claiming his mouth in an ardent kiss. The hunger they had for each other was enormous and their tongues tried to conquer and consume in a desperate attempt to make up for all the lost time and unspoken longings. There was no tenderness in this embrace of warriors, only infinite desire and a sprinkling of revenge. Hands grabbed both golden and black locks in an attempt to bring their faces even closer, to deepen this union, to be as entwined with each other as possible.

Then Radu broke the kiss and looked deep into the black eyes of the one who had stolen his soul on a bloody, muddy battlefield on that enchanted October five years back.

"I want you so badly!" he said, almost out of breath now.

"Then have me already!" came the impatient reply as Bogdan turned onto his stomach, pushing himself up just a little.

"In due time, my dear."

"It's past due time already, M'lord."

"So submissive for somebody who was commanding me to have him mere seconds ago." Radu's fingers gently caressed the proffered opening. "I think some soothing is in order first," he said, pouring some lavender-scented oil and spreading it gently over the now bare sensitive skin.

Bogdan was so aroused that he thought he might release himself there and then. He closed his eyes and felt his lover scooping a strong arm under him, lifting him up so that he could rest on hands and knees, all while coming up behind him. The moment when he would at last be filled would not be far away now, even though it felt as if he had waited an eternity for it.

"I know you are eager, but we need to do this slowly," Radu said as he inserted his calloused finger, earning a pleasure-filled growl for his troubles. He then gently started to move inside the handsome young man, stretching him little by little with his digit, while the rest of his hand was caressing the captain. As he felt his lover pushing against his hand, Radu inserted a second finger and started to thrust in and out, in and out, all the time mindful of the sounds his ministrations were producing.

"I will come like this if you don't fuck me already!"

"And that's bad?" Radu asked, in a playful voice.

"Damn it, Radu, just..." He could not finish his sentence, because quite suddenly he felt a large cock slam into him. It slid in rather easily, but, startled and disconcerted by a small stab of pain, Bogdan lost his balance and landed flat on his stomach. To his surprise, Radu had anticipated this, and his right hand had cupped his throbbing prick, saving it from an unpleasant impact.

"I'm sorry," Radu said and motioned to pull out, but Bogdan reached his hand around and held his lover in place.

"No, it's fine. I want this. More than anything in the world." He tried to rise a little, but felt the warm weight of his ruler holding him down.

"Don't. It's more comfortable for you this way."

"I don't need you to spare me." Bogdan was panting now.

"I'm not." The King again pushed inside his subject, closely observing his body language. It didn't seem to hurt, so Radu resumed his thrusts, gently at first, then less and less delicately, until his relentless slamming resulted in a loud and explosive orgasm on his part, white seed bursting forth before dripping out and down Bogdan's hairy thigh.

"Forgive me," he said, pulling out and rolling on his side to look at the beautiful face that was now flushed.

"What the devil for?" Bogdan asked, out of breath.

Radu placed a finger on his mouth. "Do not call *him* in such a heavenly moment. I'm sorry I was not more mindful of your pleasure."

"Are you looking for praise on your bed skills, or what is this about?"

"I simply wish you would have found your release as well. I lost sight of that."

"It would be worth it to let you believe that and make you feel guilty for it, but…" The young Turk lifted himself a little so that Radu could see the shining, sticky proof of his pleasure on the mattress.

"You do enjoy toying with me, don't you?" Moldova's ruler asked with a smile as he pulled his beloved's face toward him for yet another blissful kiss.

"I still want *to know*," Bogdan said, before meeting his sovereign's lips.

"No," was the simple answer he received once their mouths parted.

"Why not? Why can't you tell me why it was so important to choose this name for me? What does it mean?"

Radu smiled and, getting up, went over to the small basin to wash himself. The young captain kept him in his sight, admiring the muscled body and the confidence of his stride. He wondered how he could get his answer and have some fun at the same time. Watching the cleansing ritual and what the cold water was doing to the beautiful thing between his lover's legs gave him the perfect idea.

"How cruel to treat it with such chillness," he said and, going over to the basin, bent down on his knees and gently suckled on the soft flesh.

Radu shivered. "What are you doing?" he asked, swallowing the knot that was now in his throat.

"Warming you up," came the simple reply.

Before he could protest, the king again found himself in the sweet captivity of his captain's capable mouth. The sensation was amazing and Radu truly felt as if he had died and gone to Heaven. It was unreal to him that he could finally have this with the captor of his heart and mind, his very soul. Soon he felt he was ready to explode again and, finding support from the wall behind him, he used his hands to gently push his pleaser away.

"I don't want to come in your mouth," he said, and immediately all movement stopped, while dark eyes from below, both with a wicked gleam in them, shot right at him.

"But you do want to come, do you not?"

"Yes, but…" He could feel that it was a trap, but could not yet figure out what said trap was.

"Good," Bogdan replied calmly while his hand started to stroke up and down the giant tool, until the irregular gasps let him know Radu was close. That is when he suddenly stopped.

"What the…?"

"Now, if you want release, M'lord, you will tell me what my name means."

"You sneak!" Radu exclaimed, frustrated as his lover moved his hand farther away.

"What will it be? Shall we let this beautiful arousal go to waste or will you simply come clean as to why you chose to call me thus?"

"What makes you think I won't bend you over right now and put my arousal to good use in ripping apart your adorable little ass?"

Bogdan got up and kissed his frustrated lover's lips.

"You won't do that because I will say no, and you would never force yourself on me. Now," he continued while his hand again started to caress the pulsating cock, "why don't you tell me and then allow me to make you oh so very happy?"

Radu tilted his head and asked, "All this time, why did you not just ask another?"

To which Bogdan replied, softly, "I wanted to hear it from your own lips."

The King sighed and nodded. "It means...*gifted by God*," he whispered, surprised that he had finally given away his personal secret. Immediately, Bogdan's lips were on his while his hand moved rhythmically, squeezing until the warm seed spilled between them, dousing them both.

"Now then, was that so bad?" Bogdan teased, but the flash in the other man's eyes made him take a step back.

"Not as bad as payment for what you did shall be."

"I assure you that it has been paid for in advance."

"Are you trying to escape retribution?" Radu asked with a smile, and pulled his lover back into his arms.

"I would not dream of it, M'lord."

The Moldovians returned victorious to Putna, stopping at Neamt Monastery on their way to pray for those who had passed and to give thanks for the aid they had received in battle. The King also gave thanks for a very special gift.

REDBONE'S MAN

Xavier Axelson

The mutton was rare, charred on the outside, silky pink inside, and the dog would eat first. The dog and Redbone's man always ate first, but tonight only the dog sat beside their leader. The men watched enviously as the beast came forth and bowed its head before the meat. A low growl warned against any fool coming between it and the meal, and its eyes glittered in the firelight like black embers, its jaws snapping menacingly when the meat sizzled and spat.

"The dog will eat!" Redbone's voice boomed above the growl of the dog.

The men moved closer to the fire. With Redbone nearby, the dog would not harm them—or so they hoped. "Eat, dog!" Redbone commanded, and the dog did just that.

It tore the choicest piece of mutton from the flames and savaged the meat as though it were alive. The men closest were sprayed with hot fat and hotter saliva as the dog ate, but none dared move or wipe themselves clean.

Redbone's laughter mixed with the dog's brutal consumption as the winds carried the sounds away from the fire.

"Dog, go!" Redbone came closer to the fire. "Men, eat!"

The dog remained by Redbone's side as though savoring the fear of the men.

Redbone lifted his massive arm and pointed. "Go!"

The dog pulled the nearly stripped haunch of mutton with it as it slowly backed away.

The men descended on the remaining meat, but only after Redbone positioned himself between them and the cur, which watched the men and chewed on the mutton bone from off in the shadows.

Later, sated by the meal, Redbone lounged by the fire. The dog returned and sat by his feet, the mutton bone between its massive paws. The flames dwindled but still crackled, and Redbone stared into its heat. Rumors of a savage warrior clan coming from the West disturbed Redbone. He'd seen smoke rising along the horizon, and when they captured a man lurking in the nearby woods, Redbone sent his man to spy. But now his man had not returned. It'd been weeks. His man never failed, but perhaps this time...

Voices broke in on Redbone's thoughts. The men were telling stories of battles past and reveling in their numerous victories.

Redbone looked down and found the dog staring back at him. He scratched the beast's head. Then, as though this gesture decided some question, Redbone sat up.

"Bring the prisoner!"

The men fell silent.

"Now!" Redbone bellowed and kicked at a man who stumbled before him. "Bring me the prisoner!"

The dog lifted its head and howled.

Redbone got up and disappeared into his tent, the dog following close behind.

Camus, Redbone's second in command, pushed a large, muscular man to his knees.

Redbone regarded the man and then looked at his lieutenant. Behind them, the dog snarled.

"Axe," Redbone ordered, and another man, Nos, brought forth a mighty instrument of horror, the symbol of his people's strength. The blades dragged behind him in the dirt.

The man on his knees did not so much as lift his head.

Redbone grabbed the axe handle with such force that Nos lost his footing and fell down before the dog. The beast swiped at him with its claws the way a cat toys with a bird.

"Dog!" Redbone shot a menacing look at the animal.

Nos scrambled to his feet and retreated behind Camus.

Redbone approached the man kneeling before him, while Camus jerked the man's head back by the long, dark braid that hung to his waist.

Redbone touched the man's throat. "I'm going to kill you with this axe." He lifted the terrifying weapon and regarded the fine curves of its double blade.

The man's eyes widened, but he did not flinch. Redbone admired the fine lines of jaw and neck. The prisoner couldn't be older than twenty turns of the wheel, and his skin, yet unblemished by battle, tempted the warrior king.

"Strip him," Redbone ordered and watched Nos hold the man down while Camus stripped his crude wool garments. Once naked, the man stared defiantly at his captor.

"The demons of Blackmouth will have you," the prisoner cursed.

Redbone smiled. "I do not fear demons."

The man laughed. "All men kneel before Blackmouth, even savage fools."

Redbone's smile widened. "You speak strangely. Where have you come from?"

When the man didn't answer, Camus struck him in the face, blood spraying from his nose.

The dog growled appreciatively.

"West," the man grunted, red dripping down his chin.

"What does the West want from Redbone?" Camus demanded.

The man laughed but said nothing. Camus struck him again. This time the man hit the ground, hard.

Redbone ground his foot into the man's head. "Speak!"

The dog curled its lips back and salivated, while Camus and Nos stared at Redbone expectantly.

Redbone's brutal instincts were at odds. What if this western clan held his man captive and that's why he hadn't returned? Could they trade hostages?

The prisoner's laugh grew louder.

What if they'd already killed his man? Redbone's eyes widened with rage. He'd disembowel every one of them and feed them to the dog. No longer indecisive, he heaved the axe over his head and brought it down across the man's neck.

Blood spurted up and spattered. The head rolled away from the body.

For a moment, silence filled the tent. The air reeked of blood. Redbone dropped the axe and laughed as he breathed it in.

"Dog!" he yelled as he backed away from the still corpse. "Go!"

The dog seized the body of the man and dragged it from the tent.

Later, when the fire died and the moon came from behind the clouds, Redbone awoke and opened his eyes.

A shadow, followed by a slight movement, drew his attention to the tent's opening.

"Come!"

The tent flap billowed. Redbone smelled ash and blood and man, all of it intoxicating, familiar. His cock swelled beneath his sleeping furs and he licked his lips in anticipation.

"A warlord comes from the West," a voice whispered.

"So be it! Let him come! Let him die!" Redbone replied and fell back onto the furs, his prick straining toward the tent roof. It arched impressively from a nest of copper-brown hair and pulsed with a powerful need. The rigid flesh twitched as though possessed by an unseen force, the foreskin sliding back, exposing a glistening, meaty head. Redbone's own pungent scent mixed with the intense aroma coming from the whispering shadow.

For a moment, no reply came, but then the figure of a man, lean yet powerfully built, emerged from the darkness, his face revealed in profile. "He is called Highwind and he is powerful."

Redbone watched as the man, his man, came closer. The scent of blood intensified. "No more warnings from you." He reached up from the floor and stroked the man's calves, then dug his fingers into the muscular flesh. "Come," he commanded, which he'd done so many countless times before.

The man got on top of Redbone, who reached around and cupped the proffered ass. "I've waited too long for you," he grunted.

The man responded by backing his ass against Redbone's cock. He reached behind himself and stroked it until it seeped pearly fluid.

Redbone writhed beneath the man, arched and thrust as his cock was toyed with. "I want to fuck you," he said, his voice now gravelly.

The man laughed and clutched Redbone's bull-sized balls and tugged them until Redbone raised a hand to strike him. Again the man laughed.

He let go of Redbone's sac and grabbed his fist instead. "You wouldn't live to see it through." The man slid down Redbone's body until their lips touched.

The kiss, at first passionate, turned insistent. The man reached down and clasped their cocks together and stroked. Redbone clawed the man's back and uttered primal grunts through their kiss until the man pulled away.

"Now," the man exhaled, wiping saliva from his mouth before reaching back to slick his hole.

Redbone watched his massive cock disappear inside the man's ass. Slowly, his body relaxed and then tensed again as the man slid off him. "More," he growled.

The man lowered himself again and moaned when he took more of Redbone into his depths.

"More!" Redbone demanded, and this time when the man removed himself, Redbone clasped his hands on the man's hips and thrust him down to the coarse bristles of his crotch.

The man gasped and hit Redbone square in the jaw. This didn't stop him from taking Redbone's cock and settling onto its demanding, exploratory fucking. He rocked back and forth on it. "Harder," he insisted, panting all the while, sweat flinging off his brow.

Redbone complied, bucking and plunging deeper with each thrust. Soon their motions matched and the fucking became singular, a moment of dual pleasure melting together by their need for each other.

"Come!" Redbone barked as he rammed and slammed even harder.

The man clutched Redbone's thighs and stroked his cock furiously, matching the deep pummeling of the mammoth prick inside of him.

Redbone's eyes widened as a smile spread across his face. "Come on me," he growled.

The undoing of their fuck came seconds later. The man's first shot hit Redbone's forehead, the second spraying his burnished beard. After that, Redbone only felt the hot shower of come as he closed his eyes and unleashed himself into the warm cavern coddling his cock. When the final gush of seed ebbed, he arched his back and clung to the man.

After, when the world came back and the memories of blood and war settled between them, Redbone got up. The man followed and they left the tent together.

The night cloaked them as they left camp and sought the waters of a nearby stream. They bathed, but didn't speak. When Redbone settled by the water's edge, the man approached. Redbone stroked his thigh and said, "You were gone too long."

The man remained silent.

"What does this Warlord Highwind want with me?" Redbone asked as he reached over and thumbed the man's furry balls.

"It's unclear," the man simply whispered.

Redbone released the man's balls and looked up. "Unclear?" He raised his voice. "You stay away for weeks and come back with nothing?"

The man shook his head. "I did not— "

"I wait, the men wait, the dog waits for you!" Redbone pushed him away. "I thought you were dead!"

The man flinched. "I did everything I could."

"You seed-swallowing whore-man!" Redbone heaved himself up off the ground. "Every cock in that foul western camp probably knows your mouth, and you, you dare come back with nothing to say!"

The man made as if to speak, but Redbone pushed past him. "You failed," he snarled.

The man reached for Redbone. "I didn't—"

Redbone shook him off. "Don't come back until you have something."

Redbone met one of his men as he exited the woods.

"Time to eat?" the man inquired. The savory smell of roasting hare carried on the breeze.

Redbone shoved the man aside. When he entered the camp, his men gathered around the fire.

Camus ran up to Redbone. "The men are hungry."

Several loud grumbles rose up from the clan.

Redbone didn't answer and simply strode past. The dog, guarding the entrance of Redbone's tent, got up and padded over to its master. Redbone kicked at it, and the dog cowered.

"The dog is hungry," Camus grunted.

Redbone stopped. He went over to the fire and grabbed the wooden poles used for cooking. He lifted them off the fire and swung them at the men.

"Eat!" Redbone tore one of the hares off the poles and threw it at Camus. "The battle comes and swine must eat!" He tore off another one and hurled it at the dog, then dropped the poles. They landed in a loud clatter.

The men, moved by hunger, scrambled around Camus and snatched the hare from the dirt, then grabbed those remaining on the poles. The dog tore viciously at the meat as he eyed Redbone.

Redbone's chest glistened with sweat and hare fat. "Camus!"

Camus pushed the men aside and ran to Redbone.

Redbone gazed west. "Today we fight," he growled, and strode to his tent.

Inside, Redbone stroked the blade of the axe as if it were his man's iron prick. The fires of the enemy's camp were now closer than ever. The battle would come quick and brutal; he was certain of it. He thought of his man, the way his mouth felt on his. He undid his leather belt and reached into his fur loin wrap. Hard and slick, his cock pulsed with excitement. Redbone stroked it until his powerful thighs buckled. He wanted the man, to feel his insides once again. He yanked his loin wrap down and pumped his hips back and forth. The blade of the axe, dangerously close to Redbone's cockhead, intensified his enjoyment. His balls tightened and he called out to Blackmouth and the cruel demons inside the pit as his seed sprayed the shining blade. Spent, he dropped to his knees and rested his head against the axe.

He desperately wanted his man.

* * *

The day wore on, a sense of foreboding settling upon the camp. The dog whined and restlessly paced in front of Redbone's tent. The men wrestled and sparred at Camus's insistence, hoping practice combat would undo the disquiet. Nos assembled scouting parties in an effort to learn more of their enemy.

Redbone's man did not appear.

Soon he will return, Redbone thought as he stared at the axe. He'll come back…

A deep, thundering voice broke his mediation.

"Redbone!"

He lifted his eyes and heard men shouting and weapons clanging. He sprung to his feet, grabbing the axe before emerging from the tent.

At first, Redbone didn't know where to look. His men gathered at the edge of camp, each carrying a weapon as they stared at the western hill.

Camus and Nos joined their leader, but Redbone held up his axe-free hand, and they fell back.

"Come and meet your death!" a voice boomed, echoing across the field.

Redbone shielded his eyes. As he adjusted to the sun's glare, he saw the enemy, Highwind. He flinched, for at Highwind's side was his man. His head hung down low, and when Highwind moved, his man veered unsteadily.

Redbone moved closer and saw a cruel length of barbed chain around the captive's neck. He lifted the axe and pointed it at his enemy.

"Blackmouth have you, Highwind!" Redbone bellowed.

Highwind jerked the chain and the man fell to the ground. "No!" Highwind shouted. "Blackmouth will have Redbone and his spy-whore!"

Redbone looked at his man, rage welling within him. "Men!" he shouted, then strode forward.

At first, the warriors swarmed up behind him like a nest of angry wasps, but then faltered. A shadow passed over the sun and a large hawk flew overhead, its wings blocking out the fiery orb above. When it screeched, the men cowered.

Redbone looked up. His men were not archers, were not allowed to be, and so none knew how to battle the sky beast. He looked at his axe. Its heft felt worthless.

"Give me back my man!" he yelled over the hawk's piercing cry.

Highwind came forward, and, as he did, an army descended the hill like a wave.

"For the axe, you get the whore-spy!" Highwind responded, then swung his arm with the chain outward, forcing Redbone's man to jerk violently before him. "I'll kill him, Redbone!"

Redbone moved closer until his eyes met his man's. Above them, the hawk screeched and hung on the currents of hot wind like a malevolent cloud.

"Dog," Redbone called. "Good dog, come."

Redbone heard the men parting behind him and soon felt the dog's hot breath on his legs.

The men, poised for war, their minds consumed with anxiety and battle-lust, strained under the burden of their leader's strange behavior.

Redbone looked from the axe to his man.

"Now!" Highwind demanded. "Choose!"

Redbone lowered the axe. His sweat-soaked palms slid along the handle.

But before the axe touched the earth, a shrill cry from above suspended the action.

The hawk, struck by some object, dropped, caught itself on a current and struggled to regain its hold on the wind. When it fell, the dog charged after it.

Redbone, trained on split-second impulse, saw his enemy waver. With a swift upward motion, Redbone lifted the axe and charged. His man must've sensed the slack, because just then he lunged forward and dragged Highwind to meet Redbone.

"No axe," Redbone barked as he brought the mighty weapon down upon Highwind's right shoulder.

Highwind, no weakling, but not as large as Redbone either, howled beneath the cleaving device, which caused the enemy to rush forth, shouting all the while. Redbone knew his men had now joined him, as Nos and Camus flanked his side and took up battle.

Redbone glared down at Highwind, who writhed in his own blood, the leash still clasped in his hands. "No axe and not my man either!" He lifted the infernal weapon again and drove it down one final time.

The battle proved bloody and the hill turned red with it, the air stinking foul. The men of Redbone's army glistened like terrible hell-demons in the sun—but the day was theirs.

Redbone kneeled beside his man and undid the barbed leash. "Are you hurt?"

The man bowed his head. "I have failed you."

Redbone shook his head. "Come with me." He lifted him up. "The battle is over."

With the axe over one shoulder and his man resting against the other, Redbone walked through the carnage. His warriors gathered their fallen brothers to be burned, as was their custom.

Victorious, Redbone left the field. When he arrived at his tent, the dog awaited him, a massive hawk's wing in its jaws. Redbone smiled. "Good dog."

The dog followed Redbone inside.

Later, after night came and cleansed the day of its brutality, Redbone stared at his man sleeping peacefully on the furs, the dog right beside him.

"Redbone, I wish to speak."

Redbone looked and saw Camus and Nos waiting by the tent flap.

Camus pushed Nos forward.

"Speak!" Redbone snapped.

Nos opened his mouth, then promptly closed it.

Camus grabbed something from behind Nos's back and dropped it on the ground.

Redbone stared at the bow and arrows, then up at Nos. "You learned the weapons of the air?"

Nos kept quiet until Camus nudged him.

"Yes, I learned the weapons long before I joined with you," Nos answered, his voice nervously quavering.

Redbone contemplated the odd-looking weapons. "Our men fight with weapons of the ground only. So says Blackmouth. It is our way."

"Forgive me," Nos said, bowing. "Death is all I am worthy of."

Redbone shook his head. "Not death." He chuckled. "You will teach our men how to use the weapons of the air, Blackmouth be damned." Redbone waved them away.

The men, relieved and surprised, hurried from the tent. Redbone settled down to rest, but sleep evaded him.

When the night lengthened and still he couldn't sleep, Redbone went to the stream. The woods were quiet and he bathed until his muscles stung with the cold water. When he emerged, his man waited for him. Redbone went to him. He would always go to him. Always.

The man touched Redbone's face and stroked his coppery beard. The clouds scuttled past the moon as silver light crept between the trees.

Redbone saw the pattern of still-bleeding wounds across his man's neck. He touched one and drew back as he elicited a flinch. "Does it hurt?"

The man shook his head.

Redbone kissed him and pulled him into a crushing embrace. "Come," he commanded and led him to the water.

"Blackmouth will have us both," the man sighed. "The demons await us in the fires."

Redbone drew him up in his arms and lifted him. "Not tonight." He carried the man to the water, kissing his face and wounds as he went. "Certainly not tonight."

FOR ALL ETERNITY

Rob Rosen

I woke up coughing, groggy. The walls around me, which were blurring at the edges, were barely lit by a few flickering lanterns, and the smell of incense permeated the space. My hand reached out, over, and landed on a hairy thigh. I craned my neck to the side, squinting to bring my eyes into focus.

"Zareth," I rasped, my throat dry, voice weak.

I waited, heart pounding. At last he stirred. "Stick?" he managed.

I grinned at the sound of my nickname. *Stick.* I was a big man, far bigger than most, trained to be so, bred to be so, but next to Zareth, *Stick* seemed appropriate. "Yes, my love," I replied, rubbing his leg.

Slowly he turned my way, shaking his head as he did so, trying, it appeared, to clear the cobwebs from his mind. "What... what happened?"

I gazed around us. We were naked on a slab together, the chamber small, darkness at the periphery, the air thin, but at least there was some left. In an instant, I knew what had happened. I sprang up, heart again pounding, but this time for an entirely different reason. "Hurry," I coughed. "We have to hurry. Not much time."

He stared at me, eyes wide. "Not much time for what? Where are we?"

I grabbed his hand. "The Pharaoh must've died," I replied, yanking his massive frame off the slab. "This, I believe, is the fulfillment of his promise to me…"

I'd met Zareth, long ago, in the slave quarters. We were barely men, taken from our parents as soon as the muscles showed on our bare chests. Such was the way. He shared a room with me, our cots barely a few feet apart, a small wooden table dividing us, a washing pitcher above that. This was all we had: meagerness in a temple filled with untold riches.

He was handsome, already massive even for his age. Me, I was nothing to scoff at either, but with training from dawn to dusk, I'd eventually grow to proportions that made other men cower, and rightly so.

"Why must we guard the Pharaoh?" he asked, on our first night together in that small room of ours, once our fates had been sealed. This, after all, was what we'd been trained for, what we would do until we died: guard.

I turned to him, the candle flickering in his ebony eyes. "Look at us," I replied. "Not exactly the bodies of bakers, my friend."

He smiled and stood. He was naked, hard, his cock as long and thick as a tree limb. I gulped. He crouched to the side of my cot and kissed me. He did not ask permission, though that is what he nonetheless would've received. "No," he said to me. "I know why we guard him. What I mean is, why does a god need guarding?"

It was blasphemous to say such a thing, but I'd been thinking the same. Zareth and I were two of a legion, all with the sole task of guarding Pharaoh and all that he owned. "He is a god, yes," I eventually replied, after much thought, "but a god in mortal form, and so as fragile as you or me."

He beat his chest. "Fragile? I think not." A chuckle escaped from between his full lips, the sound running through me like thunder. And then he stood, his enormous prick hovering above my head until, at last, it was buried deep within my throat.

Perhaps fragile was not the word for it, after all, I thought to myself as I sucked the come up from his huge, swaying balls.

Our cots were pushed together after that night. That is where they remained, years into our servitude to the god-king. By then, our task was to walk the temple once the moon had risen. For Pharaoh lived with his priests in a complex of buildings that stretched far into the desert, all surrounded by nearly impenetrable walls, though these, of course, never stopped those stupid enough to try and enter, for reasons of thievery or worse. And so Zareth and I were always on the alert.

We had indeed killed our share of the dim-witted who attempted to rob the temple, though none, it seemed, had ever sought to kill our master. Still, the grumblings could be heard on the desert breeze. Pharaoh, after all, was none too eager to relinquish his earthly body to rule with his kin in the afterworld. Others, it was told, now sought to rule our own world, to dethrone the long-standing ruler by any means possible.

And so Zareth and I were now doubly vigilant. If Pharaoh was killed during our watch—well, we shuddered to imagine what would happen to us. Our bodies might've been muscle dense, our chests like boulders and arms as strong as marble statues, but they were still no match for a blade of thick metal.

And yet we were men, men with desires and passions of our own. The nights were long, and with secret passageways not so secret to the likes of us, sometimes a quick break seemed best, if only for our sanity.

Zareth had worked his cock out of his uniform and was

stroking it as we walked to a wall that was not what it appeared. I pushed the stone, then the one behind it, and the wall gave way very nearly without sound, allowing us easy access to the narrow tunnel behind it. I lit the candle that waited on the other side.

These passages, we had discovered, were used by the priests, allowing them easier access to move around the impossibly large temple complex, connecting rooms that would otherwise take much longer to get to. Over the years, they were also used for spying, by the priests and, we assumed, by Pharaoh himself. Once we found access to these hidden spaces, we also found the small holes drilled into the stone, revealing the rooms beyond and their occupants.

Zareth and I had our favorites to spy on, men who found the nighttime best for their more carnal desires: men who fucked themselves with phallic-shaped candles; men who fucked each other, for women were not allowed in the temple once the sun went down; and men who simply abused their pricks until they erupted in torrents of come. All this we watched as we in turn prepared ourselves to spew, as we in turn fucked and sucked with wild abandon, hidden from the world that otherwise watched us so intently.

That fateful night was no different.

We were well within the passageway, around a corner, my eye pressed tight to the hole in the stone, Zareth on his knees, stroking his prick as he sucked hungrily on mine. I gazed upon the priest just beyond. He was a slight man, hairless, his shaved head, on those occasions when we were near each other, barely reaching my chest, but his cock, yes, his cock was a sight to see. Surely, Zareth and I had joked, his mother had been well fucked by a bull.

He was on his bed, naked, furiously pounding his meat, hand but a blur as his small ass rose above the blanket. His club of a cock rose high above his nest of pubic hair, the head fat, glistening in the light of a nearby lantern.

I moaned as my lover again took my cock in his mouth, gagging as I fucked his face and stared through the small gap in the stone. Despite the chill of the passageway, a bead of sweat trickled down my face and tickled my cheek. I wiped it away as I shoved my prick between Zareth's lips, the candle we'd taken illuminating the scene.

I smiled down at him as he stared up at me, sucking heartily as he beat the serpent that rose between his dense thighs. My cock popped out a moment later, the sound echoing around the narrow passage. He gasped for air and then asked, "What is the bull-priest up to now?"

I chuckled and turned to stare again. "He is fingering his hole, my love, fingering and stroking, as he seems to do most nights." Again I turned to him. "Care to see?"

He nodded and rose, cock swaying as he did so. By then, he'd relieved himself of all but his tunic. I had done the same. Better to waste precious moments than to stain our uniforms, we figured. In any case, he was quickly staring through the hole while I was staring at his beautiful rump, at thighs and calves rife with muscle and hair. Again I moaned as I parted his cheeks and tickled his crinkled hole.

He moaned as well, and the pace again picked up on his prick. "You can do better than that," he whispered, the words sending a warm chill to my bouncing cock.

I grinned and spanked a cheek. "You think so?"

He nodded and spread his legs wider, his ass jutting out, the hair-rimmed center winking my way. "Think, Stick? No, I *know* you can."

I spit into my hand and wet his hole. "Smart man," I purred, wetting my throbbing prick next. "Smart and handsome."

He sighed as I slowly, gently entered him, his eye pressed tight to the hole, massive chest to the stone wall. "Which is why you love me so," he said, after a sharp exhale.

I slid my way inside, the warmth enveloping me. "Among

so many other things," I panted, my arms wrapped around him now, my cheek against his broad expanse of back. "Yes."

"Yes," he whispered, belly shuddering as I advanced farther.

"Yes," I repeated, now to the hilt, our bodies at last united.

He turned his head to the side. "The priest appears close now," he informed. "Shall we all come together?"

I grinned and pushed my face away from his back, my hands now at his hips. "Is that what the gods desire?"

He shrugged and picked up the pace on his prick. "You would have to ask the priest that, Stick, but it is what I desire."

I retracted my cock and rammed it in again. "Then so be it, my love."

Out it came, for the briefest of moments, hovering like a hummingbird before I slammed in again, out and in, out and in, until his mighty legs began to buckle. Sweat now cascaded down his back as it crisscrossed his spine. Lightning sizzled through me now, my hips rocking on instinct, the sound of our lovemaking echoing down the passageway.

One final shove, deep, deep inside of him, and my cock erupted, come filling his hole before dripping out of it and down his thigh. He came a moment later, his body tensing as his head fell back, mouth agape. His aromatic load slammed into the stone, then slid down it, gathering on the dirt floor in a white pool.

"Well?" I managed to puff out.

He chuckled as he turned to look my way. "The priest will have to change his linens, I'm afraid."

"Or have his slave do it for him, but good for our bull-like friend. Even the pious should have a little fun."

He started to reply when we suddenly heard a noise. The stone walls were thick, so it couldn't have been coming through one of the many holes we knew of; it had to have originated from our side of things.

I closed the gap between us. We dressed, quickly. "A priest?" I whispered.

He shrugged and gripped his spear. "At this time of night? Doubtful, Stick. Piety has working hours."

I nodded, my spear also held at the ready as I listened again for the sound. "Perhaps a mouse then?"

Again we heard it. Louder now, more distinct. "A mouse with a heavy tread, it sounds like to me."

And still I nodded, moving toward it now, slowly, silently, my spear to my right, his to his left, the bulk of us filling up the narrow passageway as my heart picked up speed. Onward we moved, as one, always as one, united in both love and war. The sound moved away now, perhaps turning a corner as it became less distinct, fading as we sought it out.

We reached a divide, the tunnel splitting right and left. It was impossible to tell where the sound was coming from. It was almost too distant now to even hear it. Then it was gone completely.

Zareth lifted his spear and pointed right before indicting with his head that I should go left. "Be careful," I whispered.

He smiled and moved away. "Always am, Stick. Always am."

To the left I went, the sound of Zareth's footsteps quickly muffled before vanishing altogether. I crept along the passageway, my ear held up, listening for the sound again. I stopped when I thought I heard it. My heart rate doubled, not out of fear, of which I had very little, but with the knowledge of where I now was, where I was inevitably heading. After all, Zareth and I knew these hidden trails intimately.

"Pharaoh," I whispered, with a gulp, as I sped along, praying to the gods that I wouldn't be too late or that I was perhaps mistaken as to the intruder's intent.

I was running now, not caring about the noise I was making, my breath lodged in my throat as I sped through the stone tunnel, my spear clanking against the wall. Ahead I saw a dim light, moon glow. A hidden door must've opened somewhere. I rushed toward it.

"Pharaoh!" I hollered, my voice booming as I raced there. I reached the door and sped through it, eyes darting right and left, then center. I'd never been inside the god-king's chambers before. It was, after all, forbidden. I was very nearly blinded by the glint of gold, and yet my eyes managed to land not on that but the dull metal. "Pharaoh!" I yelled, yet again, the intruder's dagger already raised.

My master stirred all too late. *Fragile*, I thought. *Oh so fragile*. I did not realize my spear was aloft, did not feel it rise, feel the bone and muscle flex and move and release in one fluid motion. It was instinctual now, branded into me. I was born to guard him. This was my destiny. I heard the sound clearly enough, just the same. Heard it slice through the air, then heard it again as it pierced through flesh. *So fragile*.

Pharaoh rolled away just as the intruder gasped and toppled onto the bed, his weapon dropping from his hand before clattering loudly to the floor below. Time seemed to stand still then as the man took his last gasp, as my master stared from him to me.

"Well done," he croaked out, his hand to his still-intact chest and neck and face. "May the gods smile upon you."

I bowed. "And to you, Pharaoh. And to you."

He rose and strode toward me. He was old, yes, but still retained the vigor of youth. To be alone with a god was one thing, but to be so close to one was another matter entirely. And so I merely continued bowing, averting my gaze as best I could.

"I shall eventually join my ancestors," he said with a rumbling laugh, "but clearly not tonight."

"No, Pharaoh," I managed to squeak out. "Not tonight."

He put his hand to my chin and lifted my head. "Do you wish for something? Gold perhaps?" He pointed with his free hand all around him. It was, after all, everywhere. "Jewels?" Again his hand pointed. "Please, please name it."

And it was then that Zareth appeared, his massive frame

blocking the doorway, eyes surprised at what he was witnessing. And with my own hand I pointed his way. "Eternity, Pharaoh," I replied. "Eternity with my one true love."

"I don't understand," Zareth said as we hobbled away from the cold stone slabs. "Fulfillment? What fulfillment? What promise did the Pharaoh make to you?"

I turned to him. "Eternity," I uttered. "We must've been drugged and dragged here when the god-king died. To be buried with him meant that we'd be taken to the afterlife, to guard him..."

"For all eternity," he said, finishing my train of thought.

I nodded. "Together, for all eternity. A wish granted, yes, though I'd have preferred it a bit later than today, my love."

His nodding joined mine. "Same here, Stick. Same here." He looked around. We were trapped, clearly inside a tomb. He then scratched his head. "How do the lanterns still flicker, though?"

I stared at the nearest one. "There must be air in here still." And it was then I remembered the priests. After all, we'd spied on them enough over the years. And they didn't always abuse themselves at night; sometimes they practiced their rituals. "The body," I said. "It must be anointed over several days before the tomb can be sealed. There is air in here, Zareth. There is. But where is it coming from?"

He bent down and picked the lantern up. We stared at it, at the flame, at its gentle orange sway. "There," he said, pointing to the far end of the chamber we found ourselves in.

We raced to the wall. Tables were positioned on either side of it, jars and bowls and pitchers scattered about, the same items we saw in the priests' chambers. "They must be coming back this way. We couldn't have been asleep for more than a day or two. The lanterns still burn, so we still have a chance."

He touched his hand to his chest and smiled. "Much still burns, Stick." And then he moved said hand to the wall, feeling his way across the stones. My smile echoed his, my hand feeling the opposite way, pushing, prodding, listening for some sort of give.

"Here," I finally exhaled, many minutes later, as one stone pushed inward, another quick to follow, until a small entryway was revealed. Zareth started to push his bulk through when I stopped him. "Wait," I added.

"Wait?" he said, turning his face my way.

I nodded and reached for a jar I recognized. I poured the liquid inside onto my hand, then on to one of my lover's. I then touched the wall, my handprint remaining as I pulled my fingers away. Zareth did the same, our prints side by side.

"For all eternity, my love," I said, pushing him out of the tomb and into the cold air beyond. "Just as Pharaoh promised."

MOJAVE

Dale Chase

Battle gets my dick up. I don't know if it's the streaming bullets or gun barrels heated from the action, but it's an arousal greater than the thrill of bringing down the enemy. Best part is fucking, which is what I often do, while the battle rages. Get my lieutenant into whatever cover I can manage, this time being a shade spire. Before I can get my dick out, he's dropped his pants, and when I spear him I savor a barrage of machine gun fire.

We're presently defending the Modesto desalination plant from attack by Sacto forces who wish to claim this border facility as their own. We've mobilized a company to push them back, but it's a challenge to do this and not damage the plant.

Lieutenant Lake works his cock as I ride him, bullets striking the spire, those that miss buzzing my ear. Then I'm the one shooting. I drive a load into Lake as he sprays jizz onto the spire, all to the sweet sound of war.

When I'm done, I pull out and Lake turns to me. Amid the dirt on his face comes a smile which I take as gratitude. He pulls up his pants, and then, right there in the thick of it, pulls off his helmet and attempts to kiss me. Damn fool, but his lips are on mine, tongue prodding, and for a second I almost give way because the whole of me stirs. I hear the familiar whiz of bullets, but it's not until I taste blood that I realize Lake has been hit. I pull back, and when I let him go, he falls. I want to drop down and tend to him, but I know better. Men die in war. He looks up at me, not pleading, not anything, as I unholster my pistol. He keeps looking as I finish him with a single shot, after which I tuck my cock into my pants, zip up and rejoin the battle. I go at it hell-bent, not for Lake, as he's gone now, but to obliterate what he brought on inside me. I blast my way toward an enemy platoon near the freshwater storage tanks, my men following me in a great swarm. I feel invincible, body armor ten times strong.

The plant sits in a cove on the Modesto coastal shore. Built in 2261, it's nearly a hundred years old, so it is one of the older desalination plants, and vital to the region. Of course, one day the ocean will swallow it as it once did plants in San Diego, Los Angeles and Santa Barbara. We should be building new plants farther inland, as there is no stopping the Pacific Crawl, that ever encroaching tide, but those who have power over such things must argue and posture until the water is up to their necks. For now, a company of Mojave's best drives off northern forces while protecting the plant. I've fucked Lake once or twice each day, always with bullets flying.

The battle appears over as quiet descends. We lose forty-two men while decimating Sacto forces in bloody retribution, not only for their attempt to take our northernmost plant, but for crossing into southern territory. The border was long ago fixed as the Stockton Line, back when that city was still dry. Now underwater, it remains alive in name only.

Blood is spattered up the sides of the freshwater storage tanks when the northern forces finally retreat. Those of their men still living are quickly dispatched. I've heard there was a time when men were taken prisoner and actually treated well. I can't imagine such bother.

I sound the call to pull back to a position behind the post-treatment building. "We cut them down by half," I tell my platoon. Just then comes word there's trouble at the plant's other end where it meets the water and where the pumping works lie. Though I'd like to give my men a rest, I issue a command to approach from two sides. "Blow 'em up the ass," I add.

This platoon is made up of my specially chosen machine gunners, who are fearless in support of the southern cause. None ask about Lake's absence. If he's missing, he's dead, since wounded are not tolerated. They know Lake took a bullet from either a Sacto or me. None ask which.

We run a wide perimeter, and once in place I issue the command to charge. All hell then cuts loose, the Sactos firing in all directions, which results in them shooting a good many of their own men.

Heavy gunfire fills the air, ripping through the day and sending smoke into that relentless sunshine. As I fire my M82, my dick gets hard, the urge to fuck as strong as the urge to kill. My rapid-fire weapon lets go a stream of bullets, and when I pause to reload, I glance at the man nearest me, Toth, whose weapon looks part of him, like a steel dick. I have to force myself back into the battle, though I do give a last thought to the fallen Leon Lake, who died with my spunk inside him.

Time is lost, gunfire relentless, bodies piling up, blood soaking the ground. At last the Sactos retreat and we go after them, shooting them in the legs, as there's no armor down there. As we move forward, we finish off those who lie screaming for mercy. I allow each one a few seconds to beg before I put a bullet to his head. I kill and kill and I want so badly to come. My prick is throbbing, and though I've done it before—come in my fatigues—this time the battle ends without relief. Gunfire fades and I figure about a hundred of the enemy got away while an equal number lie dead.

As silence settles over us, I address my men. "Good work," I say, which is all the praise a commander is allowed. I find my radio man, who has anticipated me. "I have Colonel Cross for you, sir," he says. I take the phone.

"Mission completed," I declare. "The plant is secure and intact, suffering no more than bullet holes. Their casualties are heavy, ours light. Processing platoons will begin work immediately."

"Good work, Captain Garza. I want the area so clean you'd never know there was a battle."

"Yes, sir."

"Once that's done, return to base."

"Yes, sir."

I take a second to downshift from warrior, then summon my platoon leaders. "Murdoch, Parr, your men start the processing. Damon, you and Kemp get the trucks ready to go. Mauer and Leach, your men are on blood cleaning detail. Make that plant shine."

The men return a chorus of affirmatives and depart for their various assignments, leaving a lone sergeant, Miner Toth, who has no reason to stay behind other than to offer himself. My dick may have gone soft with the battle's completion, but the urge remains. "Sir," he says to indicate he's ready. I've been considering him for some time because he gets hard in the shower, soaping his dick, working himself to a come and not caring about others watching. He's well built with a rounded ass that begs attention. "Come with me," I command. "I want to check inside the plant."

"Yes, sir."

While my company works on the plant's outside, Toth and I go in a door near the processing unit. I've been in the plant many times, seeing how desal plants are a military priority, so

I know the layout includes various nooks and supply rooms. Right now I don't want some place crowded with barrels of chlorine and stacks of filters; I want some quick corner, and as we pass an accommodating nook, I pull Toth into it. "Drop 'em," I command as I free my cock. It's already stiff, and I take it in hand as the sergeant throws off his helmet and bares his bottom. As I wet myself with spit, Toth is already pulling his dick. "Lake took a bullet," I say, as Toth is no doubt wondering about my regular man. When I shove my cock into him, I tell him he's promoted to lieutenant.

"Yes, sir," replies Toth. "Fuck me, sir. Fuck me good."

Though the battle is past, I hear a roar as I go at Toth. This I attribute to blood coursing through me en route to my cock. I'm as stiff as my M82 or even the meaner multi-mag M90, which caused me to come the first time I fired one. War and sex are inseparable, and my own M82 is buried in Toth's ass.

"I'm coming," he shouts as he sprays jizz onto the wall.

"Who gives a shit," I growl as I ream his ass. Right now he's nothing but a hole for my throbbing cock, and I pump harder to drive the point home. Once I feel the rise, I go crazy, pounding him as he braces both hands against the wall. When I finally come, I drill him with all I've got, which is one hell of a load. Then I'm spent and pull out to stand bared, so that Toth can see what did him. They all want a look, and Toth is no exception. He pulls his pants up, but leaves them open, dick out. He then approaches.

"Some good fuck," he says, and I see he's wanting more. He's blond and sports the perpetual burn the fair of skin suffer, along with the resulting early creases. We're all more weathered than our years because blazing sun and unrelenting heat do that to a man. To everything. We're all getting cooked, but right now I don't care about that. When Toth presses himself to me and attempts a kiss, I'm caught off guard, and for a couple of seconds I allow him to stir me. I even run a hand down onto his dick, then catch myself and push him back. "Duty calls," I bark.

"Yes, sir," he replies. He gives his dick a pull before tucking it away and zipping up.

"You're my second now," I tell him as we leave the nook to inspect the plant. When we meet its commander, I introduce Toth and feel pride in him being full of my spunk. I can't wait to get at him again, but, as captain, I have to keep control of myself.

Our base is about fifty miles south, in Merced. It's the northernmost of four that defend Mojave, as our region is known. Bases are Victorville, the southernmost, then Bakersfield and Fresno as you come north. It's all desert. Some say water once fell from the skies. I can't imagine that, and suspect the information is false. It should be lumped in with others about cold and snow blanketing the Sierra white. How could the mountain people have lived in that? Heat is what sustains us. The Sierra people insist the stumps that cover their mountains once stood tall, like shade spires, only living. Those people are nuts. Trees, they say, but nobody believes because nobody's seen one.

A platoon guards the plant perimeter while the rest of the company works to clear the grounds. Bodies are loaded onto trucks for transport to the disposal site on our base. Once the work is completed and the plant commander agrees things are secure, we make rough camp, then head south at dawn. I ride in my personal armored truck, sitting beside Toth, while the driver, Corporal Kemp, keeps his eyes on the road. Toth sits quiet as we go along. By ten o'clock in the morning it's near one hundred degrees outside, a hundred and ten being the norm. I suspect we'll hit one-twenty today. I don't mind the heat. Sweat makes me want to get dirty, and I don't mean with grime.

"You performed well yesterday," I tell Toth.

"Thank you, sir."

"I'm sure we'll be back up there soon."

"Well, we'll whip their asses all over again, whip them until they keep north of the line."

"We sure as hell will."

I don't like that I'm talking just to hear his voice. It's his ass I want, not his mouth, unless my dick is in it, but there's something about the sound of him that gets me.

By Turlock, I've stewed myself, and it's not the heat. The air-conditioned truck is a cool eighty, thanks to its nuclear fuel cell propulsion, but I'm probably hovering around one-twenty. Urges are all over me. I want to strip Toth and feed on him, lick and nibble and suck. God, how I want to suck. Dick, tits, toes, fingers. And fuck, of course, but not right off. I picture Toth laid out naked on my bunk with cock soft, waiting for me to get it up. He's pliable and willing and I want to torture myself until I'm ready to explode. It's like stealth in battle: go in quiet, then full-on attack. I'm silent for the rest of the ride, and when we arrive at the base, I get away quick. I head for Major Mauer's office where I offer my report.

"Fine work, Captain Garza. Go get some rest. We'll meet tomorrow at 0800 with the colonels to discuss further strategy."

"Yes, sir."

"Inform your men that the rest of the day is free."

"Yes, sir."

Rest of the day is about four hours, but any time off is welcome. When I'm back in the barracks, I make the announcement, which is met with whoops. I then order it sent down the line. I've just finished when Toth comes up. "May I see you in private, sir?" he asks.

"Of course. Follow me."

My quarters are sparse, office with bunk and locker, all behind a door I can lock. It has no windows. No barracks do. I'm told windows were once the norm in buildings housing people. Hard to believe since there's nothing to look at.

In my quarters I sit at the desk while Toth stands. "At ease, soldier," I say, and he takes the position. "Stow that, Toth. You can relax in here."

"Thank you, sir."

"I'm Tom in here."

"Miner."

"So what is it, Miner?" I'm tempted to say something filthy, but don't because I can't quite get hold of this guy.

"I'm happy you promoted me, Tom."

"You said that before."

"I don't think I said happy, and that's what I want you to get."

It's a foreign word, not in use. I saw it once in a lexicon book I'd once stumbled across and know it means pleased, only more. I found it hard to accept, and am glad those words fell away. I tossed out the book, not wanting to be seen having it. In any case, now here's Miner saying the blasted word right out loud.

"It's a good word, Tom. It has meaning."

"All words have meaning."

"But some have more than others."

I laugh. "Hell they do. A word is a word with a defined meaning, nothing more."

"That's what we've been taught and I understand why that is. We're a warring society with little room for feelings, and what better way to control them than strip us of verbal expression?"

"What in hell are you saying?"

"Do you ever get a warm feeling inside? I'm not talking outer heat. We all get that, but inside warmth that's got a tickle to it. A pleasure tickle. That's, well, that's *happy*."

This annoys me no end and I think to dismiss him, yet I don't because I've known that tickle once or twice, though I'd call it a tingle. This makes me wonder if Toth is a spy who's armored himself so he can get under my skin.

"Come sit with me," he says as he settles onto my bunk. He's absent his armor now, just fatigues, which allow me to assess him better. My dick stirs as I get how he's wanting fucking, but being a lower rank can't say it right out. I sit beside him instead of making my usual move to strip and fuck. This is a first, but I'm curious now.

"You make me happy, Tom," Toth begins. "I like the promotion, but only because it puts me closer to you. I get that tickle when you're close, that happy tickle. And I get it when you're far away, too. Just thinking of you warms me inside, and it's a good thing, Tom. There's more to life than fucking."

I snicker. "There's battle."

"Okay, there's battle, but we don't fight all the time, and in those hours free of it we are simply men. Men with needs. Men with wants."

"That's fucking."

He doesn't reply. He takes my chin in hand, turns me to him and kisses me in a way I don't know. Quietly, no tongue. One kiss, then some little ones. "There's that tickle," he says when he eases back.

My chest is tight, like it can't contain the heat, and I tingle something fierce. And worse, I may like it. "Tingle," I say as I give way without consent. "Tickle to you, tingle to me, along with an ache in the gut. You call that happy?"

"Actually, Tom, I call that love."

"Another word. Shit. Why do you keep throwing them at me?"

"Because they're good and you should know them. We all should. So much has been lost in this damnable battling society."

"Oh shit, you suffer historia."

"Yes, I know, and I sustain nonetheless."

"I should shoot you here and now."

"But you won't."

"Why won't I?"

"Because love has sparked inside you. I can see it, and it will eat you up unless you give it room."

"The hell it will."

"The thing is, Tom, I love you too. It goes both ways, this loving. It's when feelings rise up and carry us away, and it can happen without fucking."

"Well, I'm not buying that. Fucking is what men do, put it to man or woman, such as inclined."

When he kisses me this time there's more to it. I get some tongue, so I fuck him, but he talks as I mount him. "It's a loving fuck, Tom. I give myself to you completely, and from you I take your all."

Why in the hell his talk stirs me, I don't know, but it does. When I come I cry out, and once done I flip him over and suck him till he blows. When I start to get up, Miner stops me. "Why rush off?" he asks. "Stop being the captain and be just the man."

"Can 'the man' wash up?"

"Okay, then come back to me."

He watches as I clean myself, and when I return to the bunk, I bring us cups of water. Miner remains lying on his side as he drinks. "You've thrown me," I admit.

"Love does that. It's not a bad thing, Tom." Here he runs a hand up my back and starts a rubbing.

"I think you're going to complicate my life," I say, and I take a drink to avoid saying more.

"I hope so."

"I don't mean in a good way."

"I know," he says, "but love is like that. The heart holds you captive, two as one."

He pulls me down to him and I kiss him gently, trying it his way. The tingle rushes through me. I forget about talk.

We miss chow, but that's not missing much. Susten has six flavors, and I'm sick of them all. Miner says he'd rather starve than let go of the now. "You're so rough," he says as he touches my cheek. "Burned by the sun, worn by battle, yet you're handsome as hell. Do you know that?"

"I don't think about it. I'm a soldier, strong and fit."

"Well, you're very striking. Looking at you makes my heart race."

"I've never talked like this," I tell him.

"Do you like it?"

"I guess."

Just then comes a knock at the door. "Captain Garza? I need to see you."

I recognize the voice. It's Corporal Sue Pratt, and I know her reason for the inquiry. She's pregnant and needs transfer. "Not now," I call out, and to Miner I say, in a low voice, "God, not now." He's fingering my nipple as I speak.

"Yes, sir," says Sue.

Women sure know how to get in a man's way, but they are fine soldiers and must be respected, as they can reproduce. They are fucked regular and pregnant often, so they rotate in and out of units as need dictates. Sue will be reassigned to Repro Camp where she'll drop the kid, who is then put on the farm to be raised under strict control, since dying babies are a concern. I've covered over memories of those years, as I was mainly being groomed for the military by a regimented upbringing. Main thing was I survived when so many didn't. If we could solve that, we'd have an army so big we could wipe out the Sactos, but we're limited, same as them. Some say it's the fouled air, others say the desalinated ocean water. My belief is it's the Susten, which is man-made. Those who suffer historia insist food once came from the ground, which is silly. One look at the vast brown landscape and you're done with that. The dying off is most likely due to shoddy work at the Susten plants, but, since nobody knows for sure, Sue being knocked up is good news.

"Pregnant," says Miner, who now pinches the nipple. "What'll it be? Ninth? Tenth?"

"Who keeps count?"

"For the good of the cause," he says.

"You keep on talking women, I'll shove my dick in your mouth."

He goes silent and I kiss him, which leads to a slow build toward the usual. But it's not as usual; the whole of me is now involved. Last thing I recall is pulling out of him and falling asleep.

"I love you, Tom," Miner says next morning as we dress. "Carry that with you."

I say nothing, as it's his word not mine.

The meeting with Colonel Cross and the others is a veritable trial. I give my report and answer about a hundred questions, of which maybe twenty have merit. The rest are posturing among the officers, which there are too many of, though I do understand they have to exercise this bullshit strutting so they'll have it down when they get to be generals. When the meeting ends around five, I find Miner, drag him to my quarters and fuck the hell out of him.

"Good meeting?" he asks as I ride his ass.

I slap his bottom and thrust all the harder, and when I've gotten off and find he's unloaded into my bedding, I roll him in the stuff and lick it off him. We then settle in for the long haul, and every time I get into him he says he loves me, which I now accept. We pass a month in this manner, days spent on military exercises, nights spent on each other.

The colonels communicate daily with the generals, who are down at HQ in Bakersfield. Those men posture even more than the colonels, so nothing much gets accomplished. We get reports on our desal and nuclear plants, as well as some Sacto activity. I've gotten Miner to stop dredging up old words.

The month's end fairly explodes with word the Modesto desal plant has been bombed by northern forces. This is a first, as there's always been an unwritten agreement not to damage the water supply, just as there's agreement to leave nuclear plants alone. Some Sacto general must have gone around the bend. Military posturing gone to hell.

"Holy shit," says Miner when I tell him in private, before I announce to the men that we'll be taking a full battalion across the border to lay waste to Sacto country.

"Are we going to bomb their desal plants?"

"That debate may go on forever."

"What do you think?"

"I hate to see us descend into self-destruction. We've done it before, and not to a good end."

"Now you're surprising me. I thought you were anti-history from infancy."

"Some leaks through, but I find it mostly suspect."

"But you've heard the country wasn't always barren, that rain fell and there was snow in the mountains and water ran free? You know all that?"

"Word goes around. What I can see is that power-craving men brought us down."

"You're quite a man, Tom."

I have no words, so I move on to present matters. "You know we're headed into what may be the biggest battle in centuries. We mean to lay waste to all they have. That may mean desal plants in Lockeford, Orland and, if we're up for it, Sacto itself. Raze them and let those who survive the battle die of thirst."

"Will I be at your side?"

"All the way."

"Then let's go."

When the generals finally settle on a plan, we've lost nearly a week, during which time people in the Modesto area are dying for want of water. Chaos descends as hordes move south, and we're not well equipped for the influx. Tents are put up to house them around the base. There's no plan as yet on what to do with them, as the local desal plant can't make any more water than what it does. I'm advised that a platoon of men must be left behind to deal with unrest in our own area.

The Sactos will be manning the border, expecting our attack. It's decided to enlist help from the Sierras, who are raw mountain people. They inhabit peaks to the east and are said to eat lesser creatures. We've no idea how they survive and don't want to know, but, in exchange for a water pipeline run up there a couple hundred years ago, they became our allies. We turn to them now, as we want to approach Sacto country from their land. We'll mass our troops in Mariposa, go up into the mountains and drop down across the border near Pinecrest, which we know to be thinly manned. Then it's through Twain Harte and Arnold and finally across the valley to San Andreas, headed toward the Sactos' southernmost desal plant. We're to begin preparations for battle immediately.

We are quick at this, as we're well practiced at loading guns and ammunition for transport, filling water tankers and stocking great stores of Susten, which, for battle, is in single-use packets. Once ready, we move out, Miner riding with me and carrying that burden of the heart that I now tote along as well. I wish he hadn't named what's gotten started between us. As we bump along in the truck, I hope he'll stay quiet.

It takes a half a day to reach the mountains. Getting through them is laborious, though our trucks can handle it. The problem is our drivers, as they've never been on anything but flat ground. One truck is lost as it tumbles down a mountainside. We stop to see if men emerge, and when none do, we move on. The wooly and rough Sierras accompany us in their own crude trucks, which look to be thrown together from scavenged parts. They are enthusiastic about our mission because they know they're kept safe by our containment of the Sactos. We camp with these mountain people, though our tents are at a distance. I don't mind when we leave them behind.

We take Pinecrest in less than an hour. Its resident force numbers are less than fifty, and having never had any intrusion from us, it has become lax. In our first battle of this war, we swarm and kill them all. We lose just two men.

At Twain Harte, we're back on the flat we know. This area, though Sacto territory, is uninhabited. Even the scratchers have left. You know a region is done when the lowest of humanity calls it quits. This works for us, and we bivouac near an untended road. We eat our Susten and enjoy water from our tankers, half the men eating while the other half stand guard. The colonels and majors meet and allow us captains to look on.

"We expect resistance at San Andreas. That's the first major outpost. Once we take that, we'll head for their desal plant at Lockeford."

Our forces stretch out for some distance, seeing how we must carry supplies to sustain us. We remain ready to fire at first sight of Sacto forces. There's no letting them get the first shot. We are the aggressors now, laying waste as they did.

The biggest battle is expected at San Andreas, so getting fired upon by hard-charging Sacto trucks near Arnold catches us by surprise. A company of theirs lay concealed in a long draw. They rise up and open fire, which sends us scrambling. In no more than a minute, we're charging, heavy artillery taking out two of their trucks right off. Machine-gun fire blazes as we fully engage.

We remain in our trucks, as do the Sactos. All are armored and equipped for battle, drivers experienced at dodging one vehicle to chase another. Gunfire is constant, and amid the smoke, we suffer jolts of shells hitting the mark. Our machine guns are fired from gun slots, and I'm heated as my M82 sends out a constant stream of bullets. Miner is beside me, doing the same, and I glance at him once to see him with teeth bared like some animal. I about come in my pants at the sight. I'm hard, of course. The bigger the battle, the greater the arousal and the more urgent the need. Miner glances at me as if he feels what I do, but then we're both back to our weapons, our war.

We take Arnold after two days of battle, driving their forces back toward their base. Once we've got them in full retreat, I command my gunners eyes front so I can fuck Toth in the back of the truck. We're silent, just the quick slap of flesh, and I know the men listen and get hard. Hell, I'll fuck 'em all if they want, but then I'm coming and it's a gusher, all while the truck races ahead, my men firing, but not like me. I slam it into this man who's got hold of me and I give it to him good, driving spunk up into his bowels as gunfire drives me harder and harder. When I'm done, I bite Miner's neck to show him I get what's between us.

I have to pull out quick because the truck stops. We're at the base and the driver calls out about a barricade. "Swarm," I call as I do up my pants. Miner turns to me, working his cock, and I watch him come. He finishes quick, zips up, and we prepare to hit the ground. I'm ready to kill them all, as is Miner, who carries my spunk.

The base is sorry looking and the barricade is no more than a couple of badly damaged trucks on their sides. This is no match for us as we swarm in all directions, firing on anything that moves. I'm fueled by having just come. Release empowers me, and I kill and kill, decimating their forces. Miner is at my side, firing steadily. Then he's falling and I stop.

"Keep on!" I shout to my men, while I remain fixed, looking down at the fallen man before me.

He lies on his back, eyes open, knowing his fate. I pull my pistol from its holster and take the aim like I've done on countless men and even women and children if they've gotten in the way. The death shot. The dutiful death shot.

I've never had such a moment as this. Killing is my job, but I can't bring myself to shoot this man. I think how it's his fault, with his words and such, how he's compromised me, yet he's the one now offering encouragement. "It's all right," he says. "Just do it."

I have to finish him and join my men. Questions will be raised if I don't, and I've never been questioned, not ever, because there's never been a need. I look down at Miner and see blood at his armpit. The bullet missed the armor by inches. I holster my gun and pull him up, get his good arm around my neck and move him into the remnants of a building.

"You can't do this," he says.

"Hell I can't."

I prop him against a wall and pull off his helmet, then his armor. The wound gushes and I put my hand over it, but this does no good. Blood surges from between my fingers.

"I'm gone," he says. "You can't linger, you can't. Follow procedure. I'm going to die anyway, so end it. For you and for me."

"I can't kill you," I cry, tears running down my face. I haven't shed them since childhood, when I was whipped for it. I don't fight it now. Let them whip me.

"Kiss me," says Miner. "And rub my cock."

I open his pants and get out his soft prick. I take it in hand and he moans. As I work him, I kiss him, gently, as he likes. Loving, as he likes. Then gunfire comes near and Miner pulls back. "Do it, Tom. If you don't finish me, they'll finish you, and I can't bear that."

I start to do up his pants, but he says to leave them open. His hand slides over to take hold. "Not a bad way to go. I love you, Tom. Now do it."

I stand, and as I hear men outside, I fire the fatal bullet amid a cascade of tears. Miner's head snaps back with the shot and my eyes close for maybe two seconds before a soldier rushes in. "Jeez, Miner's hit?" he says.

"Gone," I reply. I'm then swept into battle, rushing ahead while feeling like Miner still has ahold of me. When Arnold is at last secured, when hundreds of Sacto men lie dead, I go back to where I left him. It's quiet now and my tears are gone. I pull his hand from his dick and tuck him away, as I want him presentable for the processing team. I kiss him one last time, knowing I've lost something in this battle. I get up, blow out a sigh and head out to the men, as there's much to do, Arnold being one conquest of many.

ABOUT THE AUTHORS

BRENT ARCHER has several short stories published with Cleis Press. His upcoming novel, *Pennington's Conquest*, second of the *Golden Scepter* series, will be out soon with MuseItHOT Publishing. When not writing, Brent can be found either on stage singing or sipping a glass of wine under his grape arbor.

JONATHAN ASCHE's work has appeared in numerous anthologies, including *Wild Boys* and *Best Gay Erotica of the Year, Volume 1*. He is also the author of the erotic novels *Mindjacker*, *Moneyshots*, and most recently, *Dyre*. He lives in Atlanta with his husband, Tomé.

XAVIER AXELSON (xavieraxelson.com) is a writer living in Los Angeles. Xavier's work has been featured in various erotic and horror anthologies. Longer written works include *The Incident, Velvet* and *Lily*.

A. R. BELL is a corporate communication specialist with a degree in world literature and a master's degree in Irish studies. Bell's first literary attempts were pieces of romantic fan fiction and Bell's writing later transitioned toward historic erotica.

EVEY BRETT (eveybrett.wordpress.com) has the same birthday as Japanese filmmaker Akira Kurosawa and a fascination for Japanese history. She lives in southern Arizona with her horse and has published numerous works with Cleis Press, Lethe Press, Loose Id and elsewhere.

DALE CHASE has written male erotica for seventeen years. Her second novel, *Takedown: Taming John Wesley Hardin,* was published in 2013; her first, *Wyatt: Doc Holliday's Account of an Intimate Friendship,* came out in 2012. Dale has several published story collections and novellas while continuing to write for various anthologies.

ERIC DEL CARLO's erotic fiction has appeared with Circlet Press, Ellora's Cave, Cleis Press and other venues. His mainstream science fiction and fantasy have been published in *Asimov's, Analog, Strange Horizons* and *Shimmer,* from Ace Books and DarkStar Books. Eric lives in his native California.

RHIDIAN BRENIG JONES has herded sheep in New Zealand, taught English in Poland and run a bar on the Costa del Sol. Now settled home in Wales, he leads an adult literacy program and writes at dawn and dusk. He lives with his husband, Michael, and French Bulldogs, Coco and Cosette.

RICHARD MAY writes gay short stories, erotic and not. His work has appeared in several literary journals, anthologies and his book *Ginger Snaps: Photos & Stories of Redheaded Queer People.* Rick also organizes several literary readings and events. He lives in San Francisco, in exile from Brooklyn, New York.

RICHARD MICHAELS has appeared in three previous Cleis Press anthologies: *Best Gay Erotica, Volume 1*, *Best Gay Erotica 2015* and *Special Forces*. Recently, one of his stories was in the collection *Not Just Another Pretty Face*. His stories have also appeared in several leading gay magazines.

RILEY SHEPHERD publishes both fiction and erotica. Riley has gender, age, ethnicity and many other demographic characteristics, all of which may or may not influence the characters, points of view and situations chosen herein. But Riley doesn't consider demographics to be particularly interesting.

B. SNOW's goal as an author of gay romance is to write at least one story in every subgenre. Her published works include a paranormal Regency novella, a short novella about a time-traveling codpiece, and four anthology stories: two contemporary, one historical (pirates!) and one rip-off of a fairy tale.

SALOME WILDE (salandtalerotica.com) has published dozens of erotic stories across the orientation and gender spectrum, in genres from hard-boiled and Southern Gothic to Kaiju porn. Editor of *Shakespearotica: Queering the Bard* and *Desire Behind Bars: Lesbian Prison Erotica*, Wilde welcomes new writing challenges, of which gay warlords is certainly one.

ABOUT THE EDITOR

ROB ROSEN (therobrosen.com), author of the novels *Sparkle: The Queerest Book You'll Ever Love, Divas Las Vegas, Hot Lava, Southern Fried, Queerwolf, Vamp, Queens of the Apocalypse, Fate* and *Midlife Crisis*, and editor of the anthologies *Lust in Time, Men of the Manor, Best Gay Erotica 2015*, and *Best Gay Erotica of the Year, Volume 1*, has had short stories featured in more than two hundred anthologies.